KING AND CASTLE

King braked sharply on the corner of the square. 'I'll just be a tick. Tell me, which d'you think is the most expensive of those cars – the Daimler or the Merc?'

Such distinctions were beyond David Castle's aspirations.

'The Daimler, I think,' King decided.

He got out of his Sierra, walked round to the boot, and took out a plastic jerry can. At a leisurely pace he went back across the square and stood for a few seconds studying Billy Cato's cars. Then he unscrewed the spout of the can, splashed petrol all over the Daimler, stood back, struck a match, and tossed it on to the petrol smear along the ground. As the Daimler gushed flame, he made his way back to the Sierra. David sat very still, wondering what the hell this maniac was going to say to justify it all.

King said, 'How hungry are you?'

'Not particularly.' David summoned up his reserves of professional energy. 'Are you going to sign the paper or not?'

'I want to talk business to you.'

'That's more like.'

'Business,' said King, 'of another kind altogether.'

John Burke

KING AND CASTLE

Based on the series
created by Ian Kennedy Martin

A Thames Methuen Paperback

A Thames Methuen Paperback
KING AND CASTLE

First published in Great Britain 1986
by Methuen London Ltd
11 New Fetter Lane, London EC4P 4EE
in association with
Thames Television International Ltd
149 Tottenham Court Road, London W1P 9LL

British Library Cataloguing in Publication Data

Burke, John, *1922-*   King and castle: based on the series
   created by Ian Kennedy Martin.
   I. Title   II. Martin, Ian Kennedy
   823'.914[F]   PR6052.U644/

ISBN 0-423-01820-5

Printed and bound in Great Britain by
Hazell Watson & Viney Limited,
Member of the BPCC Group,
Aylesbury, Bucks

I

Detective Sergeant Ronald King had pushed a lot of folk around in his time. He had used people, leaned on them here and hustled them there. There were few dark tricks that he wouldn't apply when necessary. In his bones he had always known that his own time might come; but without forever looking nervously over his shoulder he had so far been able to sense when trouble was coming up behind, and had side-stepped it. Today, sitting in his police Sierra, waiting for that crooked hunk Billy Cato to come and contaminate the interior, he was not so sure. Somewhere something was wrong. He could feel it down to his hard, blunt fingertips.

King was forty-eight, and a good three stones overweight. A large part of the excess seemed to have collected round his neck in the shape of a fat column holding up his bulky head. His eyes were cold grey, when they were not bloodshot from anger or over-indulgence. His nose, like his character, had been bent from birth. King liked food, drink and money – money for its own sake, won from gambling and then lost in gambling, extorted from small-time villains and then, all too often, lost at poker or on the horses. It was what his education had fitted him for: street education in the great outdoors, and indoors the brothels and pool rooms and boxing pubs of the East End. It was the combination of knowledge about corruption and low life with an even surer knowledge of violent ways of coping with it that had furthered his career in the CID. For a long time it did not worry his superiors or the men working under his orders that while fighting villainy he had been a pretty sharp villain himself. Results were what counted. High figures of arrests and convictions were good for the Force's reputation. If the men doing the rough work collected a few personal payoffs on the side, they deserved it. Nothing would be said unless some nosey outsider noticed and started making noises. Or unless the rake-offs got so big and bad and frequent that they started to stink.

Rain drizzled down the windows of the car. Totting up winnings and losses in his notebook, King raised his head for a wary moment to look out, starting the windscreen wipers to clear his line of vision. There was nothing suspicious ahead. But he was uncomfortable.

All at once there was a shape at the passenger window. His face bleary through the streaming rain, Billy Cato leaned down and hammered on the door. King let him wait a moment, then leaned over and flipped the lock.

Cato tumbled in. He took up a lot of space and he smelt damp. It was not just because of the rain. Billy Cato always gave off a damp smell. He fancied himself as a snappy dresser and strode about with a great macho swagger, yet you kept expecting to find traces of mould on his coat collar or sleeves, just to match that sallow, slimy face of his.

'Give me a minute.' King dabbed his silver ballpoint at the notebook, musing. 'Two times twenty-seven pounds forty-seven.'

'Fifty-four pounds ninety-four,' said Cato instantly.

'Clever.'

'I was working Petticoat when I was nine.'

'Kids' stuff, Billy. I was *robbing* the bleeding stalls when I was four. Look where it got you. And look where it got me.'

Cato cleared his throat with an odd rasp. 'It's got you two hundred quid weekly, as usual, from me' – he was growling every word out separately, as if trying to pass some sort of oral exam – 'which I'm handing you in this envelope, Detective Sergeant King.'

He duly handed over the envelope. King did not open it. He did not even look at it. Every alarm bell from here back to the nick was ringing in his head. His eyes, a bit raw from a session last night, burned into Cato's. Billy Cato looked away, out at the rain, too tense and too obviously anxious to heave that door open and heave off.

6

'Why mention my name, Billy?' King kept it very quiet. 'Why mention "weekly" and "two hundred"?'

'What are you on at?'

'Are we on the air, Billy?' Before Cato could gulp out whatever words he was trying to fit together, King swung his whole weight over and slammed him against the back of the seat. He unzipped Cato's raincoat with one practised movement, tugged, reached down and found what he knew had to be there: a telltale wire coming up from the trouser front. Ponderously, articulating as carefully as Billy Cato had done, he went on: 'I do not know the meaning of your phrase "Two hundred quid weekly as usual", or why you have handed me a sealed envelope, which I am not accepting from you. This is a matter which I think I shall have to discuss with you at a later date. Now will you kindly leave the motor.'

'Sod this for a lark. I never . . .'

As he pitched out, King was out too, racing round the bonnet of the Sierra. Cato plunged for the cover of an abandoned repair shop under one of the railway arches. King got a hold on his shoulder, spun him round, and yanked the tiny UHF transmitter from Cato's groin. 'All right, who fixed you up with this?'

'I didn't want to. I never . . .'

King kneed him expertly. 'I won't ask you again.'

'CID.'

King felt very cold. So it was the way he had suspected it might eventually be.

'You want to be striped? Is that the truth?'

'Yard Anti-corruption Squad. CIB2.'

'Where are they?'

'Out there.' Sobbing for breath, Cato waved towards a ruined wall crumbling away from the line of arches. 'In a motor.'

'You'd stoop to work for that scum?'

'They got me fitted up for a right lagging if I didn't.'

'You go back and tell 'em I've been eighteen years in this Force and there's no way they can know as many angles as I know. And tell 'em not to let me catch one of 'em down a dark

7

alley. As for *you* . . .' He hammered Cato's head back against the dripping brickwork. 'Your reputation is rubbish now. That I do promise you. Twenty-four hours, and every ponce in London is going to know you work for those animals.'

'No, Ronald. No, you wouldn't. Look, on that you can name your price.'

'Not this time.'

Clawing himself upright, Billy Cato managed a threatening snarl. 'Look, Ronnie, if you talk about this I'll kill you. I mean it. I *will* kill you.'

King chopped him all the way down to the rubble-strewn floor. 'You and yours stay well away from me. Get that? Just go and tell those bastards I'm directly threatening them with a load of trouble. And that goes for you too if you ever try to lay one filthy finger on me.'

As he stormed back to the car he saw Cato totter to his feet and go blundering off towards the wall he had indicated earlier. Whoever the two were whose trap had gone wrong, they were clearly no longer interested in him. An Allegro came skidding abruptly out, over the uneven waste ground and on to the street. All Cato got in answer to his imploring wave was a faceful of mud.

Billy Cato could get very mean. King had no doubts whatsoever about that. Cato could round up some very unpleasant characters and organize some very unpleasant events for anyone who had turned against him. But that was the least of King's worries. The empty, sick feeling way down inside was nothing to do with the likes of Billy Cato, and everything to do with CIB2. What had set them off, and what would they set up next? Once the Anti-corruption boys got a tip-off and started the pursuit, they would be more persistent and more of a menace than all the Cato-type villains around Poplar laid end to end.

King did not have to wait long. First thing next morning there was a summons to the Detective Chief Superintendent's office. As soon as he entered the room he knew this was not going to be any routine discussion.

'Sit yourself.' Hinkley had a dark, glossy, vaguely reptilian

8

face. He was capable of sitting or standing very still, even when there was turmoil all round him. His calm could make everyone else uneasy. That gift had come in useful many a time. He was as corrupt as the best of them – or the worst of them – but over the years he had played it clever, played it deadpan, organizing himself and everybody within range. Now he was cold and calculating. 'Well, Ronald?'

'We've known each other a long time, Gerald.' It was meant to sound bluff and easy. It came out seedy and pleading.

'True, Ronald.'

King waited. He was offered no encouragement. The chair was uncomfortable, too small for his heavy frame. He said, 'Billy Cato comes to a meet all wired up.'

'I heard.'

King gave him a chance to add something. Again nothing was forthcoming.

'Is that all you got on offer?' he burst out. 'If you know about it, you know they didn't pin anything on me. It was a dud. They got nothing.'

'Not this time,' said Hinkley impassively.

'I think I deserve a nod, Gerald, about like who and why these bastards.'

'Nothing I can say, really.'

'A nod was what I was asking for. Sort of . . . look, this isn't CI1, it's definitely CIB2?' Hinkley offered him a nod. 'Is it something specific, or is it general things about me?' When there was no response, he said, 'Specific?' Hinkley nodded. 'Specifically to do with Billy Cato – and maybe that Northwest Hospital Group private cleaning contract?' Hinkley's nods began to come rhythmically, automatically, without any change in his expression. 'Are they far down the road, Gerald?' King studied that implacable face. They had made quite a bit of loot between them in their time, he and Hinkley. But now he was due to be screwed, and Hinkley was still there sitting it out. 'D'you really think I'm lumbered?' Hinkley nodded. 'Resignation time?' It was hardly worth waiting for that final half-doubtful, half-mocking nod. 'I'll get Cato,' King raged, pushing himself up from the chair, 'and every last one of those bastards that work with him.'

The Chief Super waited until he had reached the door, then said unemotionally, 'Good luck.'

As King plodded across the outer office, he was waved towards a telephone.

'King.' Whatever it was, he could summon up little interest.

'Mr King? Ted Windgate here – your milkman. Thought you'd like to know. Five minutes back a gent was making enquiries about where you lived. He looked a bit suss to me. I gave him Parnell Street, but I didn't give him your house number.'

Now King was interested. 'When you say "suss" . . . did he look CID?'

'No way. Kind of madman. Funny haircut, mad clobber. Hippy, sort of.'

Cato's mob, thought King. It was all coming at him at once. Billy certainly wasn't wasting any time in trying to shut him up.

'You there, Mr King?'

'Yes, I'm here. But not for long. Thanks for the call. Appreciated, son.'

Good luck, Hinkley had said without sounding as if he believed in such a thing. Well, here it came. King had not expected to have the chance of dealing with Billy's lot quite so soon. Good luck indeed.

He hoped.

Good luck was something which had long ago given up David Castle as a bad job. At first glance most people would have written him off anyway. Thin, with gangling arms and a woeful manner which was part of his make-up when he was ten years of age and at twenty-nine had become ingrained, he did not impress the world at large with any confident image, or offer even a hint of hidden depths. His eyebrows usually expressed bewilderment. His hands tended to flop about as if making excuses without knowing what he had done wrong in the first place. The fact that he could, with the most earnest philosophical concern, throw a man over his shoulder or turn him upside down with one flick of the right ankle did not come out in normal, everyday conversation. It was a talent with limited applications, after all.

In moments of self-analysis, brought on not merely by his

aikido training but by that intuitive pessimism about himself, Castle concluded that his life had for some preordained reason been scheduled for repetitive disaster. That was how it had been so far, and it seemed unlikely to improve. Each bleak disappointment was worse than the last. He ought to have grown hardened to it by now, but fate still crept up on him and dealt unexpected blows. There was little chance that the next week or month would fail to provide something more despair-inducing than the last.

Joining the Royal Navy at the age of eighteen, Castle had soon discovered that his shipmates liked neither his looks nor his nonconformity. The lower decks enjoyed the experience of kicking him about. If he wished to survive he had to learn, in spite of his idealistic disapproval of physical aggro, to kick back. At the start the concept was purely metaphorical – metaphysical, even. It soon became tough and practical. You couldn't run away on a ship, so you had to learn a way of facing up to things. The subtle art of aikido, graceful yet deadly, was a great protection, if you mastered it with skill, true dedication and true humility. David Castle had a great deal of humility to spare. At the same time there was a knot, right in his guts, of a stubbornness which he could not explain. He won a grudging tolerance as a result of what they called his expertise in karate. After a dozen attempts to explain the philosophical distinction between karate and aikido he gave up. All he could do was exhibit his aptitude when called upon. A few brisk demon-strations, and he was not called upon too often; until one night when half a dozen ratings staggering back from shore leave, drunk out of what passed for their minds, set on him and did such damage to one eye that he was issued with steel-rimmed glasses and given his discharge.

Out of the navy, Castle decided to abandon such defences. In the decent outside world his accomplishments would surely prove unnecessary. He sought a number of peaceable jobs; but did little good in any of them. Walking into one in March, he was on his way out by the end of April. Something was lacking. Then an advertisement he read in a copy of *History Today* while visiting his dentist – for there was nothing in the techniques of aikido which could actually lessen the agonies of a right raving toothache – led him into a position as genealogical investigator. It was a bit peculiar round the edges, yet compulsive. Also it was poorly paid. To get a bit more cash in hand he reluctantly took on evening classes teaching aikido; until there remained only one regular, inexhaustible pupil at his weekly sessions, and that one such a weirdo, longing only to be thrown and rolled and tortured, that Castle decided to escape before another disaster came up and clobbered him. He needed money desperately, but desperation could go only just so far.

He broke the news to the fat little creep that there would be no more lessons. Dismally totting up in his head the income he was about to discard, he promised the creature a rebate and fixed it with the girl in the office. She was not pleased. So few people ever were pleased with David Castle that he let her displeasure roll off him automatically, the way he would have let a sudden punch waste its force and graze past him in combat.

Which left him with just the one inadequately paid job. He would have to do something about that fast. Maybe there would be a sudden rush of custom, or he could work out a favourable piece rate for tracking down the relatives, inheritors and remote connections of those who had departed this life leaving it in a mess: the sort of mess that he, David Castle, could certainly have accomplished if ever he had had anything worth leaving.

Or anyone worth leaving it to.

Like his son . . .

That need was in the forefront of his mind all the time. Regaining his son, keeping his son, all needed money. He had to summon up all his philosophy to banish the agonizing thoughts of the living and return to contemplation of the dead.

Gravestones ought to be soothing. The struggle over, the pain deadened, the world blissfully discarded: everything reduced to a few carved sentiments on a chunk of marble. It was only for cryptographers like Mr Hodinett and the needy David Castle that the chiselled names and dates and farewell messages could sometimes add up to other, financially profitable messages.

Nudging his glasses up to a reasonably safe lodging on the bridge of his bony nose, Castle found himself trying to coax a useful response from the epitaphs of Herbert Cairn King, who had expired in 1937, Letty Mary King, and Wallace Arthur King, son of same.

The vicar was saying, 'I remember the Kings. I think they were the only C-of-E in the rag trade, if you'll pardon the expression.' Castle pardoned it without so much as a shrug. 'One of the family died in Bolivia, you know.' Castle did not know. 'He was spoken of as the black sheep, though with all possible charity I must say that all of them were somewhat off-white, if you take my meaning?'

'Uh-huh?' Castle did not as yet take it.

'Villainy,' intoned the vicar, 'is inherited. It runs in families. That one' – he pointed to the name of Herbert Cairn King – 'was a cunning old fellow. What one might call a Victorian Mr Fixit. As for Wallace Arthur, son of . . . hm, I remember him only vaguely. He did not inhabit this earth long enough to continue damaging its fabric in the manner of his predecessors.'

'Dead?'

'In the war.'

'Married?'

'I believe so – yes, I'm sure – but I can't say I remember her.'

'Children?' probed Castle. 'Do you remember children?'

The vicar, who had looked frail indoors and seemed even wispier in the cold light of day, dug into the dust of his windblown memories, and ventured: 'There was a boy.'

'Ronald? Was he called Ronald?'

'I think that was his name. I do think that's what it was. Oh, yes . . . and he was brought up by an aunt who . . . let me see . . . her married name was Costigan. That's it. Costigan.'

'You're sure of that?'

'Quite sure,' said the vicar doubtfully.

'Now, the big question.' Castle took it slowly and deliberately, the way he would have lured a hitherto unpromising pupil into perfecting a swift, skilful throw. 'Have you any idea where he might be living now?'

It took time. A series of misleading answers led him down a number of unrewarding alleys. One steered him into a shop in

Stepney where he offered three quid to a spotty youth behind the counter in return for information on a King or a Costigan in the neighbourhood. The lad wrinkled his nose and fiddled about with a computer at the back of the shop. Like most of its kind it produced miles of words and a lot of pale blue sparkling lines, but no name or reference of any significance.

David Castle took a break and went to call on his employer.

Mr Hodinett had once been a schoolteacher, and retained all the mannerisms of the lower echelons of that profession. Such as his own education and experience might have been, at least they had given him a shrewdness and a canny gift for exploiting other people which fitted him for his chosen business of tracing missing beneficiaries of wills and potential claimants on intestate property. Mr Hodinett's profit was rarely large even when his researchers proved successful, but there was always the hope of hitting the jackpot one day. In the meantime his commission did at any rate eke out his pension, and as time went on he found a certain dour pleasure in sifting through the detritus of the dead, the abandoned, and the greedily hopeful.

Today Castle was neither greedy nor hopeful. He had lost one source of income. Now he wanted only a small addition to this other one in order to be able to reach out for his son. He wanted it enough to urge him on, in the face of that evasive old man sitting behind the desk and looking in any direction rather than that of anyone actually speaking to him.

'Mr Hodinett, I wonder if I could have a talk with you?'

'Of course. I have been waiting to hear how the King investigation is progressing.'

'I've found a grandfather, a son, an aunt called Maraid Costigan who raised Ronald—'

'That name does undoubtedly ring an appropriate bell. So why are you not out there pursuing the matter to its conclusion?'

'I did want to ask—'

'I have an extra titbit for you. You may recollect that the testator deeded the remaining thirty years' rent of his boat-building premises to the local National Union of Seamen. We had assumed this to be the Seamen's Union in Brixham. It now turns out that the rents were remitted to a Seamen's Union on Wharf Road, the Isle of Dogs. You may enquire there if they know the whereabouts of Ronald Oscar King.'

'Right,' said Castle. He was still determined to say what he had come to say. 'Mr Hodinett, I was just wondering . . . I've been working for you now nine months, I've produced quite a few results—'

'Eleven heirs,' Hodinett acknowledged, contemplating a number of paper clips on his desk top. 'Quite promising.'

'You're paying me sixty-three pounds a week, plus a mileage allowance.' He drew a deep breath. 'I need more.'

Hodinett sat back and said distantly, 'Ah, you want to move on. You want to tender your resignation.'

'I wasn't saying that.'

'But if you need more salary, and I assure you that my partners and myself are unlikely to pay it, you would surely wish to leave us – after working out your notice, of course?'

There was only one dignified answer to that. Castle considered it, then said, 'Forget I said anything. I'm very happy with the work. I'll go now.'

Hodinett nodded acceptance and forgiveness.

David Castle tried to forget that sly face; to forget the girl, the baby, the obsessive need for money. He would do better to concentrate on the job itself. He was a hunter on the trail. Something about it fired him with an unnatural desire, at the same time as it nauseated him.

By the next morning his enquiries had taken him to a sequence of streets in Bow lined with almost identical semi-detached houses. A milkman was driving his float through the tangle. That was good news: it took a milkman or a paper boy to know every detail of featureless patches like this.

'I wonder if you can help me, mate. I'm looking for Ronald King.'

'Yeah?'

'D'you know the name?'

The milkman consulted his crate of empties. 'Yeah.'

'I'm trying to get in touch with him. Something pretty

important. D'you happen to know if he lives round here?'

The milkman hesitated, then said, 'Parnell Street. Up to Old Ford, down on your right, then three down on your left.'

'You know the number in Parnell Street?'

'Not offhand, no. Ask anyone in the street.'

As Castle nodded his thanks and left, he was mildly surprised that the milkman should be making his way towards a telephone box, but since it had nothing to do with him personally he dismissed it. The street was what counted. All he needed now was the number. He could almost have predicted this next stage: not a soul in sight, nobody to ask. He rang a front doorbell and got no reply. Then he tried another one; and another. The fifth time he was lucky. The woman who answered the door also answered his question promptly.

'Ronnie King – *that* pig?' She pointed across the street. 'Number 15. Hope you've got bad news for him. He's nothing but bad news to everyone else.'

Castle went up the narrow path and rang the doorbell. It was another of those which provoked no reply. He pressed again; waited; offered up a silent prayer and pressed once more; and was turning away when a burly man in a heavy grey overcoat came in through the diminutive front gate.

'Mr Ronald King?'

The narrowed eyes gave him a good going-over and did not look too welcoming.

'Mr King, I've got news for you.'

'Would you come through to the back garden?' The voice was as leaden as the uncompromising eyes. 'I don't want to make a mess of the house.'

Puzzled, Castle followed King towards the side of the building and along a path to a gate through a sketchy fence. Beyond lay a patch of garden just like every other garden along this street. King opened the door of a garden shed and took out the broken wooden shaft of what had once been a garden spade, still carrying half the metal blade.

'Now, let's hear it.'

'I want to talk to you about some money.' Castle brightened up. Three or four times he had seen the smiles on people's faces when he broke the utterly unexpected news about legacies they had never dreamed of. It had been a nice, warming experience. He was sure he could wash the lowering glare off even this man's unprepossessing features. 'You may be the beneficiary of some money, if you will agree to—'

'I told that garbage Billy Cato. Told him to stay away and send no one near me. Didn't the stupid sod get that across to you?'

'Mr King, I don't think we quite understand one another.'

'If I'm going down, then he's going down. I'm telling every ponce in London he's a grass. And his money isn't enough to save him. I'm sorry for you, you wet little nit, but I want you to take the message back to him loud and clear.' Suddenly King looked past Castle and braced himself. 'Hey, is he with you?'

David Castle looked behind him. Of all the unwise things he had ever done – and they were plenty – it was one of the unwisest. The wooden shaft of the spade came down hard and brutally across his head. He fell against the side of the shed, tried to push himself away, and went down on his knees.

'Mr King . . . money . . . beneficiary . . .'

The spade came at him again, along the other side of his head. He made no further attempt to communicate with the lucky legatee. It was easier to subside and wait for the pains and bright lights to stop sizzling round within his head.

Quite a meeting: not what you would call an auspicious one.

2

David Castle reached the barrister's chambers five minutes late. The cramped corridor which served as a waiting room was painted a dull yellow which had gone sour with time. David's face was even sourer. In spite of dabbing at his neck and the side of his face on the way there he had been unable to remove all the dried blood and grit which had been ground into his jaw when he hit the stone flags of King's path.

Deirdre Aitken, his solicitor, gasped, first with relief at his arrival then with something else. 'Whatever happened to you?'

'I was mugged.'

She let her head sag despairingly back against the wall. 'We're here to convince an important QC to take your case. He has to believe that *he* can convince a judge that you're Mr Normal.'

'I'm sorry.'

'And you're late. Thank God the QC seems to be late as well.'

At that moment a secretary put her head round the door and said, 'Mr Parish will see you now.' After a disbelieving glance at David's face, her own expression silently added: Abandon hope all ye who enter here.

Herbert Parish did not bother to raise his head as they went in, but waved for them to be seated. It was obviously part of his technique to put clients at a disadvantage by continuing to peruse documents until it suited him to stop. At the same time it helped cover up the fact that only at the last minute was he bothering to bone up on the case they were here to discuss.

When at last he deigned to look at them, his eyes betrayed his shock.

Deirdre Aitken said hurriedly, 'My client has been mugged today.'

Parish decided to enjoy the possibilities this opened up. 'What a series of misfortunes occurs to you, Mr Castle! Did you at any time steal the accursed emerald eye of the little yellow god?'

David glanced helplessly at his solicitor, seeking some reassurance. Her brown eyes managed to suggest a suppressed wince. She looked just as ill at ease as he felt.

'Do try to avoid getting mugged again,' Parish went blandly on. 'It is frightfully important that you look your best when we go before His Honour. Now, I must ask you some questions which I'd prefer you to answer honestly. Yes?'

David bristled, but forced himself to sit upright and look respectful. 'Yes.'

It was the same old story all over again. To David the questions were not so much enquiries as a drab summary of everything he had gone through, and gone over in his mind, again and again, so many dreary times. He had already told Deirdre every sad detail, and then dictated it all again at her request for submission to the courts via this complacent man on the other side of the desk. By now it would have become boring if it had not still been so numbingly painful.

Just over three years ago, on leave at the end of his undistinguished naval career, he had had an affair with an intense, moody, raven-haired girl. Anne was warm and intoxicating, a vital and sweet-scented change from the crudities of the lower deck. She was changeable and sometimes wildly erratic, but that in itself was part of her fascination. She was good to be with and to hold on to. He wanted to hold on all the more securely when she told him she was going to have a baby. Life was going to be different from now on. He swore he would make this work.

But Anne, impetuous and unpredictable as ever, decided she did not want it to work. With wedding preparations well under way, she announced that she wanted the baby but did not want any more of David. She assured him there was nobody else, and knowing her he believed her. It made no sense. But then maybe it had not made a lot of sense for her to get involved with him in the first place.

Still, he wanted his child – his son, as it proved. He pleaded with Anne. No, she wouldn't marry him, and no, they couldn't live together. And no, he couldn't have little Sebastian.

David did not care for the name Sebastian, but that was one of the things he would have been prepared to get used to. He went on trying to see Anne and his boy. It happened only when she was in one of her good moods. Seven times in two and a bit years he had been allowed near them. Still he would have married her. Now, in another of her swings of wilfulness, she had decided that she did not want little Seb after all. But she was not going to hand him over to his father. Her brother and sister-in-law had been married for six years and were still childless. It would be best for everyone if they adopted Sebastian.

Best for everyone except David Castle. That adoption order had to be stopped.

'Now,' Parish was saying, 'you probably think that what you're asking for is legally reasonable. But Miss Aitken will have told you, I'm sure, that there is now a body of case law on this, and it's not altogether favourable to your position.'

'Deirdre—' Warned by the knowing twitch of the QC's eyebrows he hastily amended it: 'Miss Aitken has told me that, yes.'

'Quite. Now, you state on your Court Appellate form your occupation as teacher of self-defence technique. That I understand. Also, however, a genealogist. Pray enlighten me: what is your function as a genealogist?'

'I work for Hodinett Lineage Research Limited. I help chase up the lost beneficiaries of wills, that sort of thing.'

'That sort of thing. Potential benefactors of an intestacy?' Clearly Parish understood this, too. 'What happens when you discover one of these lost heirs or heiresses?' When David hesitated, he prompted him: 'Yes, Mr Castle?'

'I say to them that they may learn something to their financial advantage if they will sign a paper giving my employers fifteen per cent of their windfall.'

'Fifteen per cent.' Parish's nose wrinkled in disdain. 'Hm. Well now, Mr Castle, the situation in summary. Your solicitor and I have read up the case law in this area, and I shall put together our legal approach. That will be one of the two elements crucial to the success of this action. The second element . . . is you.' He sighed. 'Your appearance concerns me, Mr Castle. And I am not talking about your current bruises. As I read it here, you live in a bedsit, your earnings are very low, and your genealogical job might be considered of doubtful propriety. I may decide to recommend that you delay an action until your house, if I may put it that way, is in order.' He invited an appreciative smile from Deirdre Aitken, but got none. 'Now, the brother to whom your son is to be consigned, if the mother gets her way, is a substantial farmer and landowner. The judge will be concerned primarily about the child's welfare, not about your emotional problems. I seriously suggest that before we get to court you acquire at least a three-bedroomed flat.'

David laughed shakily. 'A what?'

'One bedroom for yourself, one for your son, and one for the au pair or nanny who'll look after your son.'

'I couldn't possibly afford—'

'Then you must change your job to one with a salary enabling you to afford it.'

Deirdre leaned placatingly forward. 'David, what Mr Parish is saying is that at the time of your appearance in court you have to look like a fair proposition as a man who has the ways and means to raise his little boy.'

'So what do I do? Rob a bank?'

Mr Parish did not seem to find this at all funny.

Outside, David offered Deirdre Aitken a glum handshake and lurched off at his usual gangling gait, incapable of uttering another word. He was heading for home, but the echoes of what the barrister had said provided a depressing accompaniment to the picture he conjured up of that neglected Victorian terraced house in a run-down street in Highbury, and his own drab little room. He couldn't face it right now. He walked; went on walking; found himself on the path beside an oily canal and followed it without wanting to know where it ended, wondering whether to hang about until the pubs opened or simply keep walking until he was too tired to care about anything in this world or any other.

It was early evening before he finally summoned up the courage to head for the place he now had to look at through the eyes of a dispassionate assessor. He knew exactly how it would seem.

He plodded upstairs very slowly, postponing the moment when he would have to open his door and let himself in. When he finally made it, he found Deirdre Aitken sitting on the creaky wickerwork chair by the unfurled sofa bed, sipping a cup of tea. She looked tidier than anything else in the room, even with her somewhat unruly hair fighting its way free of a large tortoiseshell comb. David found it easier to look at her than at the tip surrounding her. For the first time he realized what a gentle, friendly mouth she had; though right now it appeared dejected, almost bruised.

'I hope you don't mind,' she said. 'I did wait for an invitation, but . . .' She smiled, shrugged. 'It didn't come. David, it was important for me to see where you lived.'

'Er . . . yes. Of course. I suppose.'

'We have to do something.'

He slumped down on the edge of the bed. 'Such as?'

'I knew you weren't taking it in. The judge will most likely ask for this . . . this place you live in to be inspected. It won't pass.' Her lips tightened, she began to sound angry. 'You've got to move as quickly as possible, so it doesn't look as if you've moved for the duration of the court case and then hope to sneak back once you've got custody.'

He knew she was right. For all the difference that made. 'D'you want to go to a pub?' It was all he could think of, on the spur of the moment.

Deirdre got up and rattled the cup and saucer on to the cluttered draining-board. 'I can't stay. I just popped by to see. Also to tell you . . . David, I'm sorry, but I'm doubtful about getting legal aid. You may have to fund the whole thing yourself.'

Something inside David Castle snapped. He heard himself burst out: 'It's totally unbelievable, really. Crazy. If I was some cheap vicious young Tory property speculator, I'd only have to toss some spare cash around and I'd be well on the way to getting custody of my son. My own son, damn it.' He steadied himself. 'Look, you sure you won't come down the road and have a drink?'

She picked up her coat. As he helped her into it, his cheek brushed against that tangle of brown hair; and it was softer than he would have guessed. For an instant she seemed to be smiling to herself – a melancholy smile that was gone as swiftly as it had come. He slipped her scarf round her neck, though not wanting her to leave.

'I've got to get my cat to the vet before seven.' She edged a few inches away from him.

'I'm going to have my son,' said David. '*She* doesn't want him. I do. That's natural justice. Anything else is unnatural.'

'So come up with a few ideas. Better still, surface a rich dead intestate relative of your own.'

'No one in my family ever made a penny.'

She touched his hand fleetingly. 'Talk to you tomorrow.'

He moved to see her out but she was already closing the door behind her, leaving the memory of that half smile in the room. David tried to wipe it away. He had enough to cope with already, without letting himself think silly things about a bright young solicitor's fading smile.

In the morning he returned doggedly to Ronald King's address. Whatever had caused that crazy behaviour the day before, he would make sure it didn't happen again. Once the strange misunderstanding had been cleared up he would give Mr King a pleasant surprise. But he intended to avoid any unpleasant surprises descending on himself.

The milkman he had spoken to before was making a delivery on the corner, right by the telephone box. David waved to him but got no reply. He went up to King's front door and rang the bell, this time keeping a weather eye open. When several attempts proved fruitless, he went round the side of the house, remembering his way all too well. The gate was open but the kitchen door was locked and there was no sign of life.

23

David trailed back to the front door. He wondered whether to scribble a note with the Hodinett telephone number on it. The policy was not recommended by Mr Hodinett or indeed by himself: it was always better to make a personal contact and wheel the lucky chap into the office to sign the agreement before he had had time to think it over or consult his solicitor.

The sound of voices drifted from the back of the house. David went down the path again, to hear radio talk coming over the fence from an open window next door.

Somewhere a car screeched to a halt and there was the slam of a door. David headed for the front of the house yet again. Halfway to the turn of the path he was confronted by a mountain of flesh and bone, a hulking great bruiser about six feet high with long arms and widely splayed hands. The hands were reaching out for David Castle.

'You were told, sonny. You *were* told, *weren't* you?'

The right hand, proportioned like a hambone, swung for David's head.

It was all too clumsy, really. Every instinct came smoothly to his rescue. The move was so easy to answer. David's foot went behind the man's ankle, his hand clamped on that flailing wrist, and the attacker's own impetus did the rest. There was a sickening thud as he hit the side of the shed; and another as David spun him gracefully across the path to encounter the side of the house.

When he left the scene of that brief encounter, the gorilla was crawling away on all fours, whimpering.

A Sierra sat by the kerb near Ronald King's front gate. King got out, staring incredulously as the moaning heap of twisted muscle and bruised shoulder collapsed at his feet.

David Castle said, 'Ah, Mr King. It *is* Mr Ronald King, isn't it?'

'Look, I told you—'

'I am David Castle of Hodinett Lineage Research Limited. I wish to inform you of something to your financial advantage.' He gabbled it out more quickly as King, in spite of the damage inflicted on his sidekick, began to move threateningly towards him. 'You have been left the sum of twenty-eight thousand pounds in a will. If you consent to sign a contract allowing Hodinett Lineage Research Limited a finder's fee, we will present you with the full details.'

Ronald King had stopped in his tracks. He still looked dazed after what he had witnessed, and his voice sounded that way too. 'Godalmighty.'

'Mr King, if you would like to accompany me to Mr Hodinett's office for a confidential discussion—'

'Get in.' King opened the passenger door.

Hodinett put on his practised avuncular beam as the inheritor was ushered into his presence. David Castle went through the equally practised routine of introduction, dramatized to make the quarry feel important without letting him get too sure of himself.

'Ah. Mr Ronald Oscar Edward King, I presume?' Mr Hodinett was a Christmas card picture of good will. 'Lucky recipient of good fortune. Do please be seated.'

Ronald King all too evidently had a suspicious nature to go with his broad shoulders and threatening glare. He drew in his breath with a sceptical hiss, and lowered himself into the chair with every indication that he did not trust its ability to support him, or Hodinett's ability to convince him.

'Let's have it, then.'

'Well, Mr King. I think the figure available to you in the right circumstances, if handled properly, will prove to be not un-adjacent to twenty-eight thousand pounds.' He pushed a form across the desk. 'This is our standard agreement. We have the information. You sign this document, and we collect our fifteen per cent only when you collect your windfall. What could be fairer?'

David had known right away that Ronald King was not going to be one of the usual pushovers. His hunched shoulders were as querulous as that chilly QC's eyebrows had been. King said, 'I'd like to know a bit more about the circs.'

'I beg your pardon?'

'I mean I don't know how big my family is. Or was. I know in some corner of a foreign field there's possibly a team of them. I mean, maybe what you've got your mitts on is an aunt who died last week, and the news simply hasn't percolated to me. If I wait a month I save divvying up your fifteen per cent.'

Hodinett shuffled papers like a cardsharp preparing for the kill. 'I can tell you that this was an uncle of yours who died intestate four years ago.'

'How about ten per cent?'

'I'm afraid our fees are not negotiable.'

'That a fact? Well, let's put it this way. Delighted as I am to hear the news, assuming it's all kosher, I want a little pause to think about it. I mean, you're saying I'm the one and only heir, so you're not likely to be going out fishing for another one, right? So there's no rush?'

At this stage, with the prey in his grasp, it was always a rush for Mr Hodinett. But he knew how to maintain that benevolent air. 'Not at all.'

'I'll be in touch.' King got to his feet. 'Just a minute, though. I'd like to have a chat with this persevering young man here.'

'Do go ahead, Mr King. We trust our staff implicitly.'

'Good. Then in confidence.'

Hodinett glowered. Objections marshalled themselves in his mind and then fidgeted into new positions. David could interpret the signs, the twitchings and the apprehensions. But Hodinett was confident the fish was as good as hooked. There would be a payoff. You didn't antagonize a catch like this.

'If you'd like me to leave my office for a moment . . .?'

'Just what I'd like.' King waited until the door had closed, then said, 'Right. He wants fifteen per cent. On nearly thirty grand that's four and a half grand, which is a lot. Presumably *you* have all the information about this business. Enough to push me, anyway. So what's *your* price?'

David knew he should have felt outraged, but in a remote way was merely curious. 'You're sort of . . . well, pretty disgusting, aren't you?'

'What about fifteen hundred?'

'I can't do a thing like that. Not to my employer.'

'What happens if I don't sign at all?'

'This organization is out a few hundred pounds, and I don't get my bit of the commission, and I've wasted my time.'

'So it's in your interest to hang around and try to get me to sign.'

'If I thought you might.'

'I might,' said King. 'Come and have lunch.'

He managed to combine politeness and insistence. He opened the door of the Sierra for David with exaggerated courtesy, saw him into the car and closed the door; but there was something in the tempo of his movements which suggested a prison door being slammed.

'How come' – he was settling himself into the driver's seat – 'you're the karate expert?'

'Aikido,' David corrected him.

'Yeah, all right, whatever you call it. The science of snapping people into bits if the fancy takes you. Very handy. But you're right into it – well and truly in there?'

David allowed himself a distant nod.

'Let me tell you something.' King swung the car away from the kerb and through a maze of streets into a square which offered nothing spectacular in itself but seemed to have acquired some expensive vehicles, including a Daimler and a Mercedes outside one pseudo-Georgian house. 'I'm thinking,' said King, 'of starting up in business as a debt collector extraordinary.'

'Funny. From what you told me on the way to the office, I thought you were some sort of policeman.'

'Some sort, but maybe not much longer. And all because of the bloke who owns those cars over there. Billy Cato – a scruffy little sod, but he can run cars like that. Did me a mischief. Debt collectors have to keep up the macho bit, you know, as the hard man. Better get some practice in.' He braked sharply on the corner of the square. 'I'll just be a tick. Tell me, which d'you think is the most expensive of those cars – the Daimler or the Merc?'

Such distinctions were beyond David Castle's aspirations.

'The Daimler, I think,' King decided.

He got out of his Sierra, walked round to the boot, and took out a plastic jerry can. At a leisurely pace he went back across the square and stood for a few seconds studying Billy Cato's cars. Then he unscrewed the spout of the can, splashed petrol all over the Daimler, stood back, struck a match, and tossed it on to the petrol smear along the ground. As the Daimler gushed flame, he made his way back to the Sierra. David sat very still, wondering what the hell this maniac was going to say to justify it all.

King said, 'How hungry are you?'

'Not particularly.' David summoned up his reserves of professional energy. 'Are you going to sign the paper or not?'

'I want to talk business to you.'

'That's more like.'

'Business,' said King, 'of another kind altogether.'

3

Even when it was still trading, the Manor Debt Collection Agency, in its Limehouse backstreet, had not been the most impressive building in the neighbourhood. Now, with a film of dust on its windows and a 'Closed' sign dangling in the glass panel of the front door, it looked even less inviting. But Ronald King saw great potential in it. He would not have started negotiations to buy it if he had not had ambitious plans for its expansion.

The last owner was at present doing time: six years to be precise, for collecing debts rather over-enthusiastically. King knew this sad fact, having been the officer who had caught up with McElroy, found there was not a big enough payoff to persuade him to look the other way, and finally shopped him. On these premises, one filing cabinet alone had details of two hundred thousand quids' worth of bought debts. King had talked to the imprisoned man's wife and, when she allowed him to get a word in edgeways between her screeches of abuse, had suggested a cosy little deal. They argued a takeover price for more than an hour, and wrangled their way to a reasonable figure of fifteen grand. Even the likelihood of raising that much had been little more than a daydream until today.

Ronald King wanted out: the Force was virtually finished with him, but he wanted the option of deciding on his own terms when and how to be finished with it. No way was he going to eke out the rest of his life on peanuts. But sweet as the idea of the Agency was, and wide as his knowledge of the Manor and villains upon it, until today he had seen no way of raising the money. A few phone calls to men who owed him a favour, and a few threats to old associates like Colin Broadley, had given him a vague hope of squeezing a hundred or two here, a regular payment there; but already there was something in the air, they were backing away from him, his handouts would cease the moment they knew he could be of no further use to them. Now, the hell with them: there was nearly thirty thousand drifting towards him.

He opened the door and gestured expansively into the grubby interior. David Castle went in, and sneezed.

King said, 'Have you got any previous?'

'Previous?'

The kid was so deadbeat, so blank, that King had a twinge of doubt about what he was likely to do. But instinct hadn't betrayed him over those CIB2 snoops who had tried to close in on him, and that same instinct told him that here and now he was on to something that would work.

He said weightily, 'Have you got a police record? The truth, now. I'll be checking.'

'I do not have a police record.'

'Okay. And you can handle yourself with that karate or whatever you call it?'

'Aikido.'

'All right, all right. And your current job is tracing people. Just like a debt collecting agency, when you come to think of it. And you're on – what?'

'Sixty-three pounds a week.'

'And you'd like more than that?'

'I need to have a lot more than that.'

'So. Would you be interested in being in my employ at a hundred and fifty a week?'

He could sense the weedy young beanpole twisting in on himself. There might not be much spare room within that spindly body, but there was surely a lot going on in there right at this instant.

Castle said, 'I'm interested in a hundred and fifty a week. But it depends on what's involved.'

'Let me tell you what an East End debt collecting agency is all about.'

King tapped the top drawer of that cherished filing cabinet, and told him: told him about pursuing local bookies' account customers; about the punk who thought most sincerely that you had only to pay the first instalment on a hire purchase motor; about a local councillor on the planning committee who hadn't been paid as promised by a less sincere local developer for favours received, couldn't pursue the matter in the courts, but as sure as hell intended to pursue it one way or another. Protection money, restaurant contracts, cut-price deals under the counter that had to be subsidized by people who had a nasty tendency at the last minute to pretend their fingers weren't in the pie or the till . . .

'Are you interested?' he concluded.

'I have to be interested. I need the money.'

'Let's go and have a bevvy, and you can tell me why.'

Over lunch in the Two Beggars pub, it was David Castle's turn to talk. He was not sly enough or calculating enough to hide anything. That clumsy innocence might be a drawback until he was properly trained in the ways of the wicked world. Right now he was naïve and honest and might have been rather fetching in his vulnerable way, if Ronnie King had not long ago lost the ability to be touched by anybody like this wet. But skilfully handled, steered by an expert, he could be converted into quite an asset.

The story of the slut who wanted to ditch her son on a childless brother and sister-in-law might have brought tears to some people's eyes. Not King's. All he saw was that a sentimental creep like this, desperate for his wailing little baby boy and equally desperate for cash, could be used.

'So you work for me,' he said, when the saga was ended.

'I'm a little worried.' You could have banked on Castle coming up with a wavering get-thee-behind-me expression like that. 'The job you're offering could land me in clink, when I ought to be outside trying to show the law how respectable I am.'

'Naturally we'll have to be careful. Very respectable all the way. Wouldn't work it any other way.'

'If . . . when . . . I mean, if . . . I mean, when would this job start?'

King, feeling the fish take the bait, tugged on the line. 'I got to resign first. When I reckon I'm good and ready, and I've wrung the final deal out of McElroy's old lady, then let's see . . . Exchange of contracts. Could be nine to ten weeks to completion. And then—'

'Too long.' Castle sounded unexpectedly decisive. 'I have to get a high-paying job in a hell of a hurry.'

'I don't know if I'm negotiable till I've got the premises signed, sealed and delivered. And, like I said, nothing starts till I jack in the Force. Might be possible to anticipate a little. But not a lot. I don't like anticipating anything in my business.'

He sized David Castle up: vague, way-out, full of scruples and self-questionings which would never have given Ronnie King a moment's anxiety; that was the way Castle was. Yet still King knew there was something there, something special which he wanted on his team.

The landlord leaned over the counter. 'Ronald, blower.'

King grunted, pushed his way out from behind the cramped table, and headed for the telephone on the wall by the bar.

'Ronald? It's Colin Bradley.'

'Yes, Col?'

'I hear from Jack that a couple of mobile mugs out of the Yard are making strife?'

It wasn't taking long for the news to get round. 'Yeah,' said King bleakly.

'Serious enough you might elbow the uniform?'

'Might be.'

'That's why you were asking for that bit extra – the "once and for all" you mentioned?' When King made no reply, waiting, Broadley said, 'I got to tell you, Ronald, it's not a runner.'

'You say?'

'Look, you're strapped for money, all right. Just to wrap it all up peaceful and friendly, let's say I could raise from five hundred to a grand a month for a limited period. Sort of retirement present, eh? But I got to see you and discuss this.'

King considered this. Things had brightened up a lot since he had tried leaning on Broadley over that cleaning contract, but an extra grand might come in handy. If it was an offer, he might as well take it.

He said, 'All right. I'll come round to the yard. Later this afternoon, all right?'

'I'm a bit busy, Ronald. On the move. You know. Tell you what: could you meet me corner of Yardley Street and Pelham Lane, outside the Grenadier?'

'When?'

'Say twenty minutes from now? Can you make it?'

'I can make it,' said King thoughtfully.

The prickles were going round the back of his neck again. Meeting in the street, that far from Col Broadley's workshops and yard, seemed an odd way of transacting a business deal of this kind. Maybe Col was getting cold feet, afraid that the two prowlers might prowl in his direction if Detective Sergeant King were observed on the premises.

Maybe.

King went back to the table. 'You'd better come along and give me some moral support.'

Castle looked surprised. Morals had not played much part in their conversation so far.

King drove swiftly and expertly through all the back doubles, knowing every street and alley and what was likely to be going on down each of them at this hour of the day. He slowed as they turned the corner into Yardley Street, and coasted along to the junction with Pelham Lane. On the far side was the Grenadier. A couple of men went in, one came out. It looked perfectly normal.

'Well?' asked Castle.

'I smell something.'

'What sort of thing?'

'A rat. Eighteen years in the Force, son, and more than a decade in CID. Those two vultures – you don't know what I'm talking about – they're overdue a swoop.' He sat back and looked down the street. Nobody was moving. Were they inside the pub, or in an alley? That offer of a grand a month had appealed to him. This meeting place didn't. 'I shall suss a little of the geography,' he announced.

'I don't know what you're talking about.'

'All will become clear.'

33

King restarted the car and drove off slowly, past the pub and round the corner. The Grenadier was at the end of a parade of dejected shops, facing an open patch of slum clearance ground. There was nobody on the waste-ground, and only an innocuous-looking delivery van parked outside one of the shops. King drove to the end of the road and turned back. Anything else? A pillar box on the corner of a side street, a telephone kiosk close to the pub . . .

'Cop those two,' he said suddenly, tightly. A tall West Indian and a broad, hulking white man with a scar down his left cheek had come out of the pub and were looking up and down the road. 'If it came to the absolute pinch,' said King, 'could you handle one if I took the other?'

'Why?'

King did not answer, but drew up by the pub and got out. David Castle followed uncertainly. King was heading for the door to the saloon bar when the two men sauntered across the pavement to block his way. At the same moment two more came round the corner. They too were obviously Col Broadley's heavies. One of them King had seen before: name of Harris, with a couple of GBHs against him.

Harris said, 'You're Ronald King?'

'*Sergeant* King.'

'Mr Broadley sends his . . . I mean, he say's he's sorry, he couldn't make it, but . . .' He very formally handed over a brown envelope. 'Contains one grand. But Mr Broadley would like you to phone him now to discuss this and further payments.'

'I'll see to it when I get back.'

'Now,' said Harris. 'This call box.'

King surveyed their faces. None of them inspired confidence or affection. They didn't know what their orders meant, but they knew what the orders were and they were going to carry them out. It was all adding up.

Harris said, 'His private number—'

'I know it.' King went into the box. Harris stood very close, propping the door open. David Castle was a few feet away, looking more perplexed than ever. King shoved ten pence in and dialled. He had the old, old feeling in the pit of his stomach. This was going to be rough, and with odds like these against him he suspected he was going to get hurt. 'Col,' he said, 'it's Ronald King. I've met a few mates of yours.'

'Yes, sorry about that, Ronald. Sorry I couldn't make it.' There was a pause, then Broadley's voice went on at a measured pace: 'Everything in order, Ronald? You did get the envelope with the grand in it?'

King groaned. How many times were they going to try this same bloody game on him? 'You don't usually call me Ronald,' he said. 'You usually call me "wack". Are we on air, Col? Are we making a sixteen-track stereo compact disc?'

There was an agitated rustle of breath. 'I don't know what you're talking about.'

'No? Col, I did not get an envelope with a grand in it. Must be some joke of yours. Some joke,' said King reproachfully, 'about me being a corkscrew. Which I do not like one little bit, Col. No way. I'm the ruler's edge.'

A hand came over his shoulder. 'I'll have that.' It was Harris, snatching the phone away from him.

'Oh, dear,' said King, 'it's going to be like that, is it?'

'Hello, Mr Broadley,' said Harris into the phone.

One of his mates was trying to reach in and drag King out of the way. There was not enough room for the manoeuvre. King found himself with his head rammed against Harris's shoulder, and heard the faint crackling of an impatient voice in the receiver.

'Harris, this is DS Enright. I want him found unconscious with that envelope tucked into his inside pocket. Leave the phone off the hook. We'll listen to progress.'

Harris let the phone dangle, seized King by the arm, and manhandled him out on to the pavement. The other three closed in. Beyond them, Castle blinked.

King felt a surge of panic. The real, bowel-twisting thing this time.

'You!' he yelled at Castle. 'I mean, it really was you who hit Kennett? I never saw the blow. You did hit him?'

The West Indian and his squat sidekick somehow had iron

bars in their hands. King, raging, tossed the envelope past them. Castle's reactions were immediate. He caught it, stared at it.

'One thousand pounds,' said King, 'towards getting your lad back. Yours if you'll help me lay waste to these bastards.'

'Okay,' said Harris, 'King first.'

King wrenched himself round towards the phone box. Harris slackened his grip, and King was free and away across the road. Two of the men were after him, but one of them went down after only three paces: David Castle had somehow stepped across his path, and done something with his elbow which produced a remarkable sort of somersault.

But Harris was close behind King. He grabbed. King ducked; stumbled on to the waste ground, and went down, his fingers closing round a brick. Harris pounced. His face met the brick.

An iron bar flailed out of the sky. King rolled aside, and heard it thump against the ground a few inches from his head. Somebody crashed into him, moaned, and crumpled over the bar. Pushing himself up, King blearily recognized Castle's torn corduroys, encasing legs which were right now doing things Fred Astaire would have envied. Two men were groaning in unison. Another was silent. One – King had lost track of which one – was fleeing for cover, over the road and round the corner of the pub.

A few pieces of paper fluttered over the battlefield. They were banknotes. Panting, David Castle was collecting them, pausing every now and then to wipe blood from the corner of his mouth. King did the same, and tried to grin. It hurt. But he thought of what Castle had told him about that legal hassle, and suspected that his precious QC would not have gone much on what had happened – yet again – to Castle's features.

'Would you believe it.' Aching in more limbs than he had thought he possessed, King propped himself against a remnant of brick wall. 'Attempted assassination – arranged by who? I'll tell you who: cops out of the Yard Anti-corruption Squad.' He stared at the telephone box, then laughed hoarsely. 'Hey, you know what? They've been listening on that blower. Hope they enjoyed the programme.'

Castle was saying urgently, 'I can't take your money.'

'Saved me from assassination, didn't you?'

'Can't take it. And also I can't wait three months to start working for you.'

'That a fact? Looking a gift horse in—'

'I can't wait. That's all there is to it. I have to start earning money now.'

King shook his head. Then stopped shaking it: the results were too dizzying.

For some reason Castle was plodding towards the telephone box. As if from a great distance King heard him saying, into the phone, 'Sergeant King has resigned forthwith.' Then he hung up.

'Just a minute, son.' King heaved himself up on to his two feet. 'What you just done? *You've* given in my resignation? What the hell—'

'I told you I couldn't wait.'

King's breath had almost been taken away by some of those murderous punches a few minutes ago. Now he was well and truly gasping.

'I'm not going to like you,' announced Castle. 'I'm only doing this for my son.'

'Yes, yes.' King managed to find his breath and his voice again. 'Bore, bore.'

'I'll work for you only and exclusively for money.'

'That's the only kind of loyalty there is. Come on' – he nodded towards the Grenadier – 'we're conveniently located for refreshment. Not closing time yet.'

They sagged into a couple of seats in a shadowy corner, where they could inconspicuously dab at their lips and knuckles and tug bits of rumpled clothing into some sort of shape. David Castle pushed the envelope towards King. King pushed it back.

'Keep the grand. You earned it.'

'It's a lot of money.'

'Think of it as your early Christmas bonus.' Reasonably tidy, King waved towards the bar. 'Two pints of lager, two Scotch eggs.'

'That'll be two pounds eighty, guv,' said the barman, prodding tongs into the glass case by the pumps.

King looked at the man's face, and knew it. He said, 'You've got a short memory, Mr Publican.'

The barman gulped. 'Oh, sorry. Didn't recognize you for a minute, Sergeant. Yes, of course.' He put the glasses and the two small plates on the bar and turned away.

Castle said, 'Hey, stop. Just a minute.' And to King he said, 'Pay. From now on everything's straight.'

There had to be at least ten answers to that, and every one of them lethal. King let the breath whistle between his teeth, then took out a fiver and handed it to the barman.

Castle smiled a boyish smile and lifted his glass. 'Happy days.'

'I ruddy well hope so,' said King woodenly.

4

By the end of the first fortnight in his new job, David Castle
was none too optimistic about the next few weeks, let alone
the next few months. He had gone through the accumulation
of files and done a lot of sums on paper and the agency's
pocket calculator, to work out how much they could hope to
collect from defaulters and how much might be expected
from potential new business. Results so far gave him little
confidence in the continuance of his hundred and fifty a
week.

Moodily he glanced around the office as he opened up the
morning mail. It made his cramped little pad look positively
luxurious in contrast. The smell, too, was disturbing. Until
recently he had not known that you could have dry rot and
rising damp simultaneously. One corner of the room was not
safe to venture into: one floorboard had disappeared long ago,
and two others tilted and shed crumbling splinters if you as
much as touched them with the toe of your shoe. It occurred
to David that his partner had purchased a bit of a lemon.

He turned his attention away from the scenery and read the
scrawl on one of the letters:

> Dear Sirs,
> I dont owe this debt what you say I do, so you lying bent
> bastards prove I do.
>
> Yours,
> Ray Mullins

David looked glumly down his typed list of names and
addresses. Ten had been struck off already this morning, one
gratefully ticked – a princely payment of fifteen quid – and one
queried for further examination. He added another query.

The next envelope had a postal order in it. The sender did not seem likely to offer rich pickings in the future:

> I enclose postal order for £4.50. About the other £1700 I've only got my Giro to live on so you can work it out, it is difficult for me to be going to pay you more.

There was a wretchedness about so many of them that struck a sympathetic chord in David's head. When the world was filled with that sort of thing, what chance did he have of doing any better? He almost preferred the blustering, aggressive letters.

> Dear Sir or Madam,
> I enclose a cheque for one hundred and seventy-five pounds in full and final settlement of my debt. You will note that the cheque is post-dated four months which is the best I can do.
>
> S. J. Smith, Mr

And there was a particularly choice one which must have been meant personally for King, if the opening was anything to go by:

> Dear bastard,
> I am going to have you done right over. I'm going to have you bankrupt. And any bent business you try, I'll get you and all for the lot.

It was unsigned. David was re-reading it with a mixture of amusement and concern when the door of his office opened, setting off a creak of protest right along the surviving floorboards.

King came in and glared. 'Do you have to park your evil-smelling rotting moped in *my* office?'

'I can't have it in the street. Not in this area. And if I brought it in here, it'd disappear through the floor.'

King looked at the opened letters on the desk. 'How's it coming?'

'Hardly at all. Forty replies to one hundred and four letters.'

'That's good. Quite a high percentage.'

'Only three,' said David, 'with cheques.'

King made a noise that might have been a wince or a belch. He went out of the room to his own office for a moment, and returned with a bottle of Perrier water, a plastic cup, and a bottle of milk of magnesia. When he had knocked back a hefty mouthful he stood quite still until he had achieved an unquestionable belch.

'I had a run-in last night with a Thamesmead Tandoori Revenge Special,' he confessed. A film of sweat oozed from his brow at the memory. 'Fall for it every time. We go sailing in, we sit at their tables, we pick out a lot of fancy names from the menu, and then they get their own back. They know we hate their guts. Out in the kitchen they grind up the cockroaches.'

'*You* may hate their guts,' said David. 'I don't hate their guts.'

'That's because you're weirder than them. You really are a spectacle. If you were walking the streets of Bangladesh a couple of their citizens in white masks would come up and arrest you as a health hazard.'

'We do seem to be out of sorts this morning.' As King propped himself against the wall, whose plaster rustled even more ominously than the floor had done, he added, 'Aren't you going to go out knocking on doors?'

'I have one or two little visits I must make. But basically my movements are restricted for a while. Unlike my motions. At the moment it's three minutes in every forty-five, increasing. Better stay near the arrangements for a while.'

David knifed another envelope open. It contained six fifty-pound notes, but no letter. He turned the envelope upside down and shook it.

King's hand was claiming the notes. 'I think I know who that's from.'

David reached for his ballpoint and poised it over the list. 'Which one?'

'Not to worry.'

'Look, if I'm also being employed as book-keeper here, no funny business.'

'And *you* look. My head's pounding like there's an alien just getting ready to burst out of it. Give me my money. Go away.'

'The best thing for a bad stomach is mint and caraway tea.'

This time it was a wince, not a burp. 'Go away!'

David surrendered. He had one call to make on a man who owed more than he ought to have done to a bookie. There was no need to feel sympathy for types like that, anyway. He could give full rein to his hunter's instincts.

'Back in half an hour,' he said, 'and then I've got early lunch with my lawyer.'

'You mean your girlfriend.'

'She's not completely my girlfriend yet.'

'Don't get technical with me,' growled King.

David wheeled his moped cautiously out of the adjoining office towards the street door. It was opened for him by a young policeman, who stood courteously aside and then closed the door behind him. David hesitated on the kerb, debating whether or not to go back and see if there was something he ought to be in on. Then he dismissed the idea, and set off.

Ronald King paid a visit to the lavatory as soon as David was out of the room. He returned only slightly improved, and regretting that there was no refrigerator in which to keep the toilet roll. The sight of a waiting policeman did nothing to cheer him.

'Mr King? I wonder if I could have a word with you, sir.'

King ushered him into the office and waved towards a chair. The young constable stayed on his feet, planted in the middle of the threadbare carpet.

'You'll have to excuse the refurbishments,' said King. 'Now, what can I do for you?'

'Well' – the young man looked shifty but knowing – 'it's a message.'

'Message from who?'

'Well, it's mainly your friends.' The constable let it hang there for a few seconds, then added, 'And Mr Hinkley.'

King began to get the drift. 'You got something to say to me,' he grunted, 'say it.'

'Yes. Well. It's like . . . well, when Mr McElroy was running this place . . . well, you know what I mean.'

'I don't know what you mean. And I'm a busy man, son.'

'Well, really, I've been sent by Detective Chief Super, Mr Hinkley. I think it's about the arrangements for Friday.'

'You *think* it is? And what arrangements for Friday?'

'Mr Hinkley said I was first to ask you to be reasonable, hear it out, and not to fly off the handle. You see, Mr Hinkley and the others have a very definite idea about the amount, and it's . . . er . . . the message is, well, to put it this way . . . it's non-negotiable.'

King felt a violent urge to return to the bog. But bleakly he said, 'What amount?'

'One hundred and fifty in an envelope every Friday morning. Cash. I collect.'

King might have guessed that the old system would have gone on working: he had once been part of it himself, and had every reason to know it wouldn't just fade away. But a hundred and fifty . . .

'Tell the Chief Super my reaction is one of stunned disbelief. I'll want to discuss this matter with him.'

'He said he thought you might,' grinned the cocky young copper. 'He said as soon as you'd had a chance to think it over, ring for an appointment.' He clumped towards the door. 'I'll be on my way, then.'

'That's a very good idea.' King was controlling his fury with difficulty.

'I'll tell Mr Hinkley that you'll be in touch.'

'Do that.'

It took King a good three or four minutes to stop shaking. Of course he ought to have foreseen this. Of course he ought to have made allowances for it in all his estimates. But now the moment had come, he found it as hard to believe as . . . well, he supposed, as his own victims had found it when *he* had been the one with his palm extended.

The pangs set off other pangs, and he set off for another trip down the passage. On his way he saw a couple standing at the desk of the blue-rinsed temp David Castle had taken on.

'Mr McElroy about, then?'

The man was in his forties but dressed in the trendy

products of a High Street store with its eyes on a somewhat He had the sort of dark, moody features which women might find attractive: especially older women, if he chose to try a smouldering glance on them.

King made a gallant effort to subdue his desire for a spell of solitary meditation in that little cupboard ten yards away. 'Good morning.' He summoned up a businesslike smile. 'My name is Ronald King. I've recently acquired this organization from Mr McElroy. Is there anything I can do for you?'

'Gadney. George Gadney.' The man peered at him, his moist olive eyes narrowing. 'Don't I know you from somewhere?'

'I don't think so, Mr Gadney. But it's a pleasure to meet you now. And . . .'

King had been about to include Mrs Gadney in the greeting when something warned him off. A closer look at the creases around the mouth and the even deeper ones not concealed by her eye make-up, and you could guess she was a good ten years older than the man. Both of them were smoothly suntanned, and should have been looking healthy and content with the holiday they must so recently have returned from. They looked no such thing.

He led them into his office and pulled the two available chairs into position facing his desk. The blue-rinsed freak outside proved surprisingly efficient in providing cups of tea.

'Right,' said King expansively. 'Whatever problem may have brought you here, do feel free to tell me the whole thing. In complete confidence.'

'He's a swine,' said the woman. 'A raving lunatic.' A fold of flesh on her throat trembled from side to side. 'He ought to be put away. I said so years ago.'

Obviously she was not referring to George Gadney, who nodded tight-lipped agreement and reached over to squeeze her knee.

King said, 'If we could begin at the beginning, Mrs . . .'

It worked. 'Mrs Midgeley,' she said. 'Katrina Midgeley. But only in name, now. And I can't wait to get rid of it.'

After that the story unfolded rapidly and, to King's jaundiced ear, all too predictably.

Mrs Midgeley had divorced her husband some months ago. She had done her best, she assured Mr King, to keep the whole procedure decent and civilized. There was agreement on the division of property and the sale of the house, with each of them getting half the proceeds when it went through. Nobody could say she hadn't been reasonable. Even when he cut up rough and started calling her all the beastly names under the sun, she still did her best to keep calm and friendly. 'Some of us have been properly brought up, some haven't.' And when the final decree came through, dear George here had taken her away to Spain to get over all the unpleasantness and the rotten taste Ernest Midgeley had left in her mouth. But what did they come back to find? After all she had done to keep things civilized – her pallid blue eyes beneath long, dark lashes implored King to believe her – what had that raving maniac gone and done?

She and Gadney were shaking their heads, still stunned at the subsequent events. The division of the marital home had been specified, and Ernest Midgeley had merely decided to take things literally. In his ex-wife's absence he had let himself into the house, fetched the chainsaw from its usual shelf in the shed, and set about cutting all the furniture down the middle: kitchen table, dining table, chairs, work-tops, and the Welsh dresser on which Katrina had kept her treasured bits and pieces of Staffordshire china.

And now he had disappeared.

King nodded. 'I see what you need. Yes. He's wrecked the place. You intended to sell the place anyway.'

'But not in that state,' wailed Katrina Midgeley.

'You'll get a loan from the bank to repair his vicious vandalism,' said King soothingly. 'You then sell the house. Recover from his share of the proceeds the loan you get from the bank. That's the ideal scenario, right?'

'But you have to find him first.'

'Quite so. Which brings us,' said King, 'to the matter of my fee. Now, finding your ex is going to be no mean task. If you remember his car number—'

'Oh, I remember it all right,' said Mrs Midgeley venomously.

'Something to start with, anyway. Then if I track him down I have to put the screws on him to sign a bundle of papers along the lines of the aforesaid.'

'Right,' said Gadney. 'I tell you, though, he's stubborn.'

'Meaning it may be necessary to run a little bit foul of the law.'

'Go on,' said Gadney grimly.

'It's got to be two grand.'

Mrs Midgeley wailed again. 'Two grand?'

'Dear, take it.' Gadney was squeezing her knee again, beginning to caress it in a coaxing rhythm. 'We've got to see this through. If *I* find him and punch him, it's back inside for the duration. Leave it to the experts. If Mr King does all he says he'll do, I think the fee's reasonable. I do know about these things.'

Yes, thought King, I'll bet you do. He had not seen the face before, but he had seen the type. If that was what turned Katrina Midgeley on, hard lines: it was her lookout – and her money.

'Leave it to me,' he said.

Having shown them out and made a belated but blissful sortie to the lavatory, he jammed two ideas together in his mind and found that they rang quite harmoniously. Some kind of deal had to be made. He knew that; and fancied he might turn at any rate part of it to his own use. An appointment, the constable had suggested. The sooner the better.

Such appointments rarely took place within the walls of the police station. It was always better in the open air, far enough away from any official building or official vehicle which might be bugged.

King opened up without wasting time: 'Tell me I've heard this all wrong, Gerald. A Friday manila of one hundred and fifty . . .!'

Hinkley beamed benevolently, playing the part for any passer-by of the eternally helpful senior police officer on friendly terms with the public. 'When McElroy was in business,' he said amiably, 'what was *your* arrangement with him? What did you get, and what did you put in the general kitty?'

'You know all this, Gerald. You know it all.'

'Yes, Ronald. And now you're the one who's becoming a professional debt collector. The man who once had your business is in jail – you put him there – which shows it's a sensitive line of commerce. You know you need all our support on the occasions that are bound to come up when you start distributing a little rough with the smooth. You run a night-club, or a bookie's, or a debt collecting agency around here, then you need friends. Us. It's a tradition.'

'Tradition?' exploded King. 'Like Eton and Harrow, now?'

'No, Ronald. More like Strangeways or Parkhurst, or whatever institution your friend McElroy got sent to.'

King stared down the road. It would have been great to make a gesture – a two-fingered one at Hinkley, for starters, and then a defiant stride away down the pavement and round the corner, off into the unknown. But this slimy lizard, hoisted up on its two hind limbs, would not have been impressed. King forced himself to speak levelly, man to man, or reptile to reptile.

'All right. It's on. I can see it has to be. But I want a few favours. For which, I presume, I won't be billed extra.'

'An example?'

'My company,' said King, 'is currently handling the case of some nutter who's created a ruckus round his ex-old lady's real estate. Name of Ernest Midgeley, and he's got a W-registered Volvo estate, and I've got the number. Could you try DVLC?'

Hinkley studied him for a cold-blooded moment, then took out a notebook and began to jot down words and numbers. 'See what I can do. Anything else?'

'Has he got form?'

'I can check.'

'The client, the wife, goes round with a male Caucasian gorilla, fortyish. Name of George Gadney. CRO?'

Hinkley wrote the name down.

King, suddenly bitter, snapped, 'You'll do that for me, will you, Gerald?'

'All part of the service, Ronald.'

King watched the Chief Super stroll back towards the snug, smug security of the station, where everything could be cosily arranged, everything manipulated – unless you made such a serious blunder and took such a wrong path that it led you way out into the cold.

He turned back towards the premises of the Manor Debt Collection Agency. There was nothing like being self-employed. Nothing, he tried to assure himself, like it.

Deirdre Aitken had been sitting on a bench in the Inns of Court gardens reading some legal papers. Her furrowed brow was not in keeping with the vulnerable, youthful waywardness of her eyes and lips. Professionally she had trudged her way through the treacheries and disillusions of human conflict; for herself, she was still virtually untouched, untried. When she looked up and saw David approaching, her smile was shaky and undisciplined. She crammed the papers any old how into her briefcase, and he took it from her. Without consultation and without any specific decision they strolled away.

She said, 'I'm going on holiday.'

'Where?'

'A secret address.'

'Abroad?'

'I'm telling no one.'

'Oh.' He was stricken by the thought that she would be away, just when he might most want to talk to her; and listen to her.

'Except you,' she said, looking far away, 'in case next of kin have to be informed.'

'What are you on about?'

She dabbed at a strand of hair, and another one drooped over to tangle with it. 'It means I'm not telling my partner. He's too inquisitive. Too bright by half. So I've told him I'm off to Romania, to a hotel without a phone.'

'Isn't Romania high up on tourist lists of places not to go?'

'I'll never know. I'm going to spend three weeks at home sitting on my derrière working out what I'm doing with my life, my career.'

He caught her arm. 'I'll tell you what you're doing and what you're going to do. You're going all the way, if necessary, to the House of Lords, and you'll win custody of my son. For *me*.'

Somehow it did not seem to be the response she had been looking for. 'I think I'll go to Romania,' she said fretfully.

'You're in a funny mood.'

She went on staring into infinity, not turning to include him in her gaze yet reaching out for him with words, a bit breathless, ready to drop the whole thing and pretend it had never been said if he failed to grasp it. 'I do feel a bit funny. Funny peculiar. So pay no attention if I invite you to join me in Romania. Translated into English, that means Dollis Hill. Bring a bottle.'

She couldn't mean what he vaguely, gropingly realized she did mean, could she? 'What do they drink in Dollis Hill?' he fumbled.

'Turpentine.' They stopped of one accord. From a distance they must have looked odd, standing a couple of feet apart, both facing in the same direction but not moving on or turning aside. Strangers, uncertain what to say – uncertain if they even knew each other. 'I like you,' said Deirdre in an abstract sort of way. 'I want you to spend some of my holiday with me. Including some lunches.'

'And dinners?' he contributed.

'An evening or two. A night.' It was little more than a whisper. 'Maybe a dawn, maybe a few daybreaks.'

It was warm and real, and a pulse was beating inside him, and he didn't believe it but he was damn well going to go right ahead and accept it anyway. They had lunch together, and it was a good one, but he hardly tasted it and five minutes after it was over he would not have been able to describe one item on the menu. What was good, especially good, was what they went on to say, even though most of it was what they didn't say in so many words. It was the best news he had heard in about fourteen and a half years.

If it was true. If there really was a place such as Romania within his grasp. Or Dollis Hill.

Before he went back to the office, they kissed. Very quietly, on a street corner, with nobody bothering even to turn and snigger. It was the first time.

He floated back to the street in which the agency stood;

floated on a cloud of benevolence. He drove the moped with automatic skill, slowed correctly on the corner, and steered with lyrical elegance towards the front door of the premises.

It was only when he had come to a halt that he realized there was no need of a front door to admit his moped to its inner parking slot. Half the front of the building and a large section of its side were open to the elements. A bulldozer appeared to have tried to gobble up a number of bricks and the furniture closest to the outer wall. A low loader was at this very moment endeavouring to winch it out without bringing the whole upper story down. In David's absence, something more briskly destructive than dry rot or rising damp seemed to have had a go at the building.

King was standing well back, looking up purple-faced at the damage. The temp, patting her blue rinse into a semblance of order, was shrilly announcing that she was leaving this very minute.

'What happened?' David demanded.

'Work it out,' snarled King. 'A bulldozer came into reception to make a complaint, that's what happened, isn't it?'

'Oh, Mr Castle.' The blue-rinse was overjoyed to see the less aggressive of the two partners, a fresh audience for her dramatic account. 'There was this dreadful little man came in, said he had a message for Mr King only Mr King had just gone out, so I couldn't help him and then he said: just tell Mr King greetings from Vince Grob – I mean, *what* a name for anybody to have! Vince Grob.'

'Greetings from Vince Grob?' David looked unhappily at King. 'Is there going to be much of this?'

'Much of what?'

'The business is hardly on its feet, and all at once we're kneecapped. I mean, is there much more of your past around to catch us up at regular intervals? Bulldozer now, gift-wrapped with greetings from dear Old Santa Grob. Arson next week, you reckon, team of snipers the week after?'

'This is my business,' said King. 'You've got your job, you get on with it.'

The irresponsible logic of all this, thought David in a dismal slump after that brief interlude of euphoria, was that if such events kept happening, he wouldn't have a job because King wouldn't have any business to conduct anyway. Maybe he ought to go back and un-tender the resignation he had handed to Mr Hodinett, who in any case had not seemed to understand him.

'This isn't a debt collecting business.' He waved indignantly at the shattered façade. 'It's anarchy. Sheer amateur thick-ear stuff.'

'Have you finished?'

'I fancy I *am* finished.'

'Listen. We've got a big commission. And it's not in postal orders, or post-dated cheques. It's all properly set up between myself and a client with the wherewithal. If you have the time of day,' said King with heavy sarcasm, 'would you care to accompany me to an address I have just been donated? And you'll see a home that has suffered a great deal more aggravation than this place.'

5

'Yes,' said David Castle, 'I do see what you mean.'

The kitchen was a shambles, a triumph on the part of an undo-it-yourself maniac. Nor would any of the other rooms in the house have passed as worthy examples of modern design for living. The standard lamp in the sitting room lay in two neatly equal lengths. Not just the bookcase but a cross-section of books had been sliced through. The banisters up the stairs were a little more ragged: it must have been a bit tricky to make an exact division at that angle.

'All yours,' said King. 'We recover enough money from this lunatic to institute repairs. And help towards our own repair bill, right?'

David studied the devastation, and agreed that steps towards restitution were in order. 'It is morally reasonable,' he said aloud, 'to get this character who ruined this house to pay for it.'

King raised his eyes to heaven. 'A miracle! Judgment of Solomon!'

'I'm not so sure about that. Solomon was the one who started this idea of chopping things down the middle. Only with him it was babies.'

King grimaced his distaste, took out a notepad, and tore off the top page. 'Here. Courtesy of the local coppers, an address for the man we seek – his sister. She's supposed to be a hard nut, so watch she don't tilt at you with a smack. Registration on Midgeley's Volvo has been transferred to her, maybe to keep it safe when someone catches up with him. Which you're going to do.'

David took the slip of paper.

'And this,' said King. 'Recent Kodak on Ernest Midgeley,

provided by ex. Taken when they were still on speaking terms – he's actually smiling.'

David stuffed the items in his shirt pocket, tried to do up his jacket button but felt it slide through his fingers. It bounced twice and disappeared under a frayed edge of bisected carpet.

King said sourly, 'Some of our turnover is going to have to be earmarked for kitting you out in clothes that won't turn the stomachs of our clients. Okay. On your moped.'

The address on the paper was that of a launderette in Camden Town. A young man with clothes which should have been inside one of the machines rather than on him was dreamily watching the swirling patterns in one of the tubs. David's glance at the young man raised his spirits considerably. King had nothing to complain about: nobody could have looked as bad as that specimen.

A supervisor in a white coat was inspecting the interior of a washer at the end of the line.

'Miss Midgeley?'

'I am not.'

'Can you tell me where I can get hold of her?'

The supervisor straightened up and appraised him. She sucked in her lower lip. 'Friday, elevenses, comes in here,' she said non-committally. 'We make a cuppa. She pays me wages.'

'D'you know where she lives?'

'I do not.'

'It's really her brother, Ernest Midgeley, I'm trying to get hold of.'

'Are you? Well, I don't know him.'

The line between indifference and blank hostility was a fine one. David tried again. 'You don't have a home or business address for Miss Midgeley?'

'No. Why should I? As long as I get me wage, that's all I care.'

Somewhere in the back, beyond a door at the end of the launderette, a door slammed. The woman's expression, too, had slammed shut. David knew he would get nowhere by asking any more questions here.

He had parked his moped close to the corner of an alley running down beside the launderette. As he sauntered towards it, abstracted, turning over possibilities in his mind, he almost walked under a car swinging out of the alley. A sharp, savage yet scared face peered at him and looked away. The car swerved. The car was a Volvo. The ferrety face was that of Ernest Midgeley.

David tried to wave at him; shouted, put out one hand, and was knocked back by the lurching rear bumper. The Volvo accelerated away down the road. David had no illusions about following it. Leaping into the saddle of a mettlesome horse and giving chase to a stage coach was one thing. The saddle of a moped and the driving seat of a Volvo were quite another.

He rode back, disconsolate, to the office.

King's Rover was at the kerb – the far kerb, a safe distance from any wall which might decide to fall down.

'Hop in. Got something to show you. You can tell me on the way what progress you're making.'

David told him. King snorted. But he seemed to be concentrating most of his attention on something else. They drove through Battersea and onwards to Lavender Hill. King waved a hand airily at some of the larger terraces as they turned off the main road.

'Quite an area, huh? It's got everything.'

'What do you mean by everything?'

'The rich, for one thing. Lords and earls, what you call old money, in nice big flats, down that edge of Battersea, Prince of Wales Drive. Round here, the yuppies – very good debt collector-wise, always getting in over their heads financially; buying a yacht when they can't keep up the payments on their sink disposal units. Then it's got the villains, tending towards the southern borders with Clapham.' Before David could ask what on earth this had to do with the King and Castle set-up, King concluded, 'Robbers, muggers, rapists, debtors, the lot.'

The Rover turned a corner past a row of shops, slowed, and came to a halt opposite a vacant window. The shop premises were empty but not derelict: the façade had been smartly repainted not too long ago, and the glass was not yet flyblown.

'Who are we supposed to be hunting this time?' asked David warily.

'You know that three hundred cash in an envelope? No note, no name?'

'Go on.'

'Came from an estate agent who once got in some trouble I found out about. I truly believe,' said King with a mocking, puritanical rasp in his voice, 'there is no sector of our society more bent than estate agents. Well, my estate agent benefactor is handling this.' He waved expansively at the shop. 'Double-fronted premises. This is a good trading street. Low overheads, A1 state of repair. No dry rot, wet rot, rising damp. No bulldozers.'

'Is that guaranteed in the lease?'

'This is a different scene, son. Different Manor. Look, I can't fight it, not back on the old patch. I can't fight Chief Super Hinkley and my former colleagues and their hundred-and-fifty-a-week demands. It's not that it's unaffordable. It's more the humiliation. It's them saying to me I'm just another punter on their Friday rounds. If we stay in Barnet Grove I have to pay. But if we move here . . . *there*' – he pointed again to the shop, proprietorial already – 'we don't pay.'

'Bonuses all round,' insinuated David gently.

'Look, son, there's a four-bedroomed flat over those premises. Didn't your brief tell you to get a three-bed accommodation to satisfy the judge? Put simply, would you move here, live above the works? I'll throw in the flat rent-free.'

'And a ten per cent increase in salary?'

'Bollocks!' King was outraged. 'Come on, now . . .'

David grinned. 'I'll grab it. Have you seen the flat? It's okay?'

'Whatever its conditions, it'll be the Savoy compared, by all reports, to the hovel you live in.' King held out a fiver. 'Five ones for a cab. I'll stay on here and see the estate agent. You get on with finding Midgeley and earning your keep.'

'Right. And, all joking apart . . . well, I mean, thanks.'

'Yes, yes, all right.' King was beginning to go red in the face and to sound at his angriest. 'Now push off and use your loaf. And whatever else you need.'

David found a cab and went to reclaim his moped. It took him back to the launderette, because there was nowhere else to start from. And the speed at which Midgeley had come out of there in his Volvo surely meant something.

The shop next door to the launderette was a cluttered grocery store, run by what was obviously a hard-working Pakistani family. There was an appetizing tang of spices as David plodded into the shop, squeezing between shelves and piled-up boxes utilizing every square inch of exploitable space. He picked up an orange and showed it to the woman behind the cramped counter, which nevertheless managed to accommodata a small, wide-eyed child as well, watching David as if his job were to check and record everyone who came into the place.

'I wonder if you could help me,' David said casually as he paid over the money for the orange. 'I'm trying to contact the lady who owns the launderette next door.'

She shook her head. 'It's not a lady who owns. It is Mr Shah who own laundry, my shop, and number eleven.'

David felt a twinge of hope. 'Where can I contact Mr Shah?'

'At number eleven.'

Number eleven proved to be a chemist's shop, with a tiny counter backed by a glass cubicle housing a dispensary. A dark young girl offered David a spontaneously hospitable smile, looked him frankly up and down, and waited to find out which of many ailments he thought they might prescribe for.

'Is it possible to speak to Mr Shah?' he asked.

She went behind the partition. A few seconds later a middle-aged Pakistani appeared.

'Mr Shah?'

The answer was a grave nod.

'I wonder if you could help me. I wanted to contact the lady who rents the launderette premises from you – a Miss Midgeley, I think?'

'Who told you that?'

'Well . . . I mean, what?'

'You have got it the wrong way round,' said Shah curtly. 'I am renting my premises from her. She owns this shop, the launderette, the greengrocer's.'

'I wonder if you could give me her address?'

'Why?'

'Some urgent business.'

'But perhaps,' said Shah with shrewd dignity, 'she want her address private. I do not know you from Eve or Adam.'

'You're not going to tell me?'

Shah's dignity was even more chilling. 'No.'

Fate did not seem to be nudging events along in David's direction. Cold shoulders were all that appeared ready to greet him. He picked his way carefully out of the shop and looked along the line of buildings on the far side of the street. There were two boarded-up houses, the end of what must once have been a chapel of some kind, a converted shop with thick lace curtains shrouding whatever it might be now, and a news-agent's.

That was a promising lead. He crossed the street and went into the newsagent's to buy a packet of cheap envelopes. Before emerging into the outside world again he folded one blank envelope, put it inside another, and licked the outer flap. When he returned to the chemist's shop he held it out politely.

'Now what d'you want?' said Shah.

'Miss Midgeley's brother did a lot of damage to his ex-wife's house. I work for the said ex-wife and some of her friends.' He paused to let the implied threat sink in. 'They are extremely angry. In this envelope are the details about what these friends propose to do about the matter within the next few hours. I think Miss Midgeley would be very pleased to get this letter and maybe avoid a lot of problems happening.'

He tossed the letter on to a packet of headache tablets and walked out before Shah could start asking questions.

The moped made a lot of noise before he could get it started. He made sure of that. Then, revving madly, he racketed away down the street. When he crept back to the corner of the alley he was wheeling the moped, and shoved it under the overhang of a sagging, green, corrugated iron gate with a fringe of barbed wire drooping over it.

He waited. He had a hunch that he would not have to wait long, and he was right. Mr Shah, who had probably spent a couple of urgent minutes on the phone, came hurriedly out of the shop door and dived into a Ford Escort. David reckoned he could match the pace of a vehicle of that age and in that condition. He gave it a good start, then set off in pursuit.

The journey did not take long. Shah's Escort slid in beside a row of nineteen-thirties' semi-detached houses, backed by a tangle of allotments and an overshadowing railway embankment. David drew up with bags of room to spare, and waited again. And again he knew it would not be a very long wait. Shah was moving far too fast, in a panicky trot, to keep anybody waiting long. He dashed up a flight of steps to a side door at the end of the row of houses, and disappeared inside. Beyond him David could see the edge of a back garden, some broken fencing leading on to the allotments, and the railway line.

Somebody came and stood in the open doorway – a tall, broad, tough-looking woman. Shah was at her elbow, waving at nothing in particular, just waving. Then he left; and she held the two enevelopes in her two hands, separating them, turning them over and looking out furiously across a stretch of nothingness.

David, glowing with what he would have been reluctant to acknowledge as sheer downright smugness, let Shah go and folded his arms philosophically.

A man came out on to the side steps. From that distance, David could see better without his glasses; and observed that the man was undoubtedly Ernest Midgeley.

Midgeley hurried down the steps and along the side of the garden towards a caravan in the bottom corner.

David found a telephone box fifty yards away, and dialled the office.

'I've found him.'

'The address?' When David had dictated it, King said, 'Stay put. I'll be there. Or maybe we'll all be there. I think this will go off with a bigger bang if I can get Gadney and Mrs M in on the act.'

David stayed put as instructed. There was little chance of Midgeley making an escape without him spotting it. Not that Midgeley seemed to have that in mind. He was hosing down the side of the caravan – maybe planning a holiday trip in the not-too-distant future? – and whatever his sister was cooking up, it was taking place out of David's line of vision.

The important thing was that Midgeley was still there.

David was getting into the swing of things. He was so alert that he felt rather than heard King coming. Even before the sound of the Rover throbbed round the end of the street he was on his feet, tucked away in a gap of an arid hedge, eating the orange he had bought but watching for King to appear. The other two were new to him, but they fitted the impression King had given him of the blowsy Mrs Midgeley and her swarthy gallant – if gallant was the word, which on first sight David thought it wasn't.

King edged closer to him. 'Where?'

Before David could direct his gaze in the appropriate direction, Katrina Midgeley had let out a shriek. Teetering up on to her toes to look over the hedge and through a gap in the garden fence, she screeched, 'There he is, the bastard.'

'Wait, dear, wait.' Gadney was not quite ready for the rough stuff; but the ex-Mrs Midgeley was on her way like a heat-seeking missile. 'We'll do a kind of circular pincer-style movement' – he tried to assert his authority over King and David Castle – 'coming round from the rear.'

'You're the client,' King granted.

'Don't underestimate him. That's why I want us to work in concert. He's a terrier. Vicious temper. He'll fight, I'm warning you.'

'My friend here,' said King loftily, 'is a punch-up specialist like you never saw. A hard man.'

'Really?' said David.

'Come on. Let's go.'

They were quite a way behind Katrina Midgeley when she stooped to pick up a brick from what had once been designed as a rockery but had recently been neglected. She let out a war cry which curdled David's blood, and had the same effect on Midgeley when he spun round and saw the avenging fury heading for him. He ran; but found there was nowhere to go except over the fence and then a succession of wire fences dividing the allotments.

The brick hit his neck. He howled, went down, got up, and vaulted the first fence with a vigour which David had to admire.

Midgeley was fast on his feet. There was no denying it. But his ex-wife was fleeter than might have been expected, and she was closing in. King, panting, dropped behind. Gadney was in no hurry to get involved in any hand-to-hand combat. David, putting on a spurt to catch up, found himself intent on saving Midgeley rather than capturing him. Once the one-time love of his life got her hands on him, there was a danger of her collecting more debts than any man could possibly have owed.

Another banshee howl was added to the confusion. Midgeley's sister appeared at the top of the steps, wielding a broom. She came down at the charge, hurling Gadney aside, and would have risked impaling King if the broom handle had had a sharper end. They crashed to the earth as she stormed on, past Castle.

Katrina Midgeley, momentarily baffled as Ernest sprang desperately over a coil of wire, turned to meet the impact of her sister-in-law. She seemed to relish the encounter as much as she would have done grappling with Ernest himself. Grasping one end of the broom, she wrenched it to one side so that Miss Midgeley went reeling off balance. Then she resolutely pushed her face into the ground, kicked her, and turned her attention back to the ex-husband.

Midgely vanished. But only briefly. He emerged from an allotment hut with a murderous-looking pitchfork on his arm, slanted like a lance.

It was a deadly moment. Midgeley was hyped up, scared and angry and raving mad. His face was as venomous as it must have been when he carved his way through his old home. King, puffing his way to his feet, stayed where he was. Even Mrs Midgeley wavered, hissed something obscene, and took only one step forward.

David Castle moved in.

He took it very slowly. Slipping his jacket off, he wound it round his right arm in case he had to block a jab from those savage prongs.

There was an odd hush. It was as if they had all seen the

silliness of it, and it was all going to be brushed aside and forgotten. Everyone would pretend nothing had happened and nothing was going to happen.

Midgely advanced on David. He thrust the pitchfork forward. David sidestepped. Midgeley's foot slid, he swung violently, and lunged again. David backed away, taking his time, taking it easy, luring Midgely on to soft earth and then edging to one side. Midgeley, uncertain, made a wild rush in the hope of pinning him into a corner of the wire. David stepped back, felt the wire against his ribs, and then went forward. He grabbed the pitchfork with his right hand, Midgeley with his left, and then hurled the pitchfork as far as he could. Off balance, Midgeley scrabbled to get a hold on David's shirt. David punched him neatly and unfussily on one side of the head. Midgeley went down. With one bound David retrieved the pitchfork, danced back, and pressed the handle across Midgeley's throat to hold him down.

'What's this about?' Reality sobered Midgeley up, sobered him into breathless terror.

'I think you know. If not, Mrs Midgeley now has the opportunity to explain.'

Imploringly Midgeley pushed at the handle. David slackened it off a fraction.

'That slag!' Midgeley sobbed. 'All me adult life I paid every bill on that bloody house – mortgage, electricity, gas, repairs, everything. I *loved* that house. Then she says she's going off with her boyfriend, and I'm to be a good boy and sign all the bloody papers without making a fuss . . . and at the end of it all, a judge comes along and says I'm entitled to just half me house – half me *own house*!'

'I've got my own problems,' said David, out of breath. 'With women. And they're a lot worse than yours, friend.'

As Midgeley sat up, rubbing his neck, King planted himself beside David. He had a document in one hand, a ballpoint in the other.

'Here. Put your signature on that. No need to read it. Just sign it.' As Midgeley confusedly shook his head, King hauled him up, banged him against the fence, and sat him down on a

61

water butt. In the background Gadney and a tousled Katrina had just finished subduing Midgeley's sister. Gadney swaggered over to join King and Castle, trying to put on a good act. King said, 'Here, you witness it.'

Midgeley scrawled his name. Gadney added his own. King took the document before anyone could raise any queries.

Gadney said, 'You'll get paid. No problem.'

'I know I'll get paid,' said King. 'It's part of the document.'

'I know it's part of the document. I'm just saying that because I mean it. I've every intention of paying you. It's just that I've got one last piece of business with you.'

There was a jagged edge to his voice. King must have got a warning resonance, for David saw him cock his head on one side.

Gadney stepped closer. 'It came to me – who you are – or who you used to be. You were that double-bent bastard Sergeant King, put my cousin Robbie away for a four stretch.' Before David could intervene or King could put up a protective arm, Gadney had punched in a neat upper cut. King went down. Gadney walked off, to take the arm of the adoring Katrina.

David made a move to intercept him, but King, struggling up, gasped, 'Leave him. Why waste the effort? We'll get the fee.' He took a few steps and leaned on David's shoulder. 'We'll get the fee, and we'll get away from the East End and every rotten memory. Come on, let's visit Lavender Hill.'

Watching Gadney and Mrs Midgeley leaving, David said, 'Looking back, I think I'm on the side of our friend Midgeley here rather than those two.'

'In this game you're on the side of whoever's paying the money.'

It had been an eventful day. Now it was a quiet, reflective evening. But David was beginning to feel a sort of anticipatory tingle. It might just possibly be an eventful night.

Deirdre was clearing away the plates from a table on to which two tall red candles cast a restful glow. They had eaten; he had told her about the flat over the new premises; and there was no denying the sensation of well-being which was warming him inside – not all of it as a result of Deirdre's culinary accomplishments.

Looking out of the window into the deep twilight, with a scattering of lights here and a sudden new cluster there, he said, 'Are those the Hills of Dollis?'

She closed the door to the tiny kitchen and sat on the sofa studying him. 'I know you're thinking about the law case.'

'Not right now I'm not.'

'And I know,' she persevered, 'I said I'm on holiday. But it's a holiday to do some real work on the process of getting your son for you.'

'Thanks.' He was watching the light in her eyes now, and the way her lips formed each syllable, provocative even when she was talking dry facts.

'I'll have to go back with some good stories for my partner about Romania.'

He pointed out of the window. 'There, across the water, you can just make out the lights of Sevastopol.'

'Is that true?'

'Later we'll go into Bucharest, try and find a phone to dial your office. And fail.'

'Sadly. Then we'll have dinner – shashlik and devilled goats' eyes.'

'Washed down with eighteen litres of Bull's Blood.'

'That's Hungary, you twerp. Then we'll drive to Constanta, on the ocean.'

'Yes, we'll need some place to throw up after the goats' eyes.'

'It'll be midnight on the Black Sea,' she said dreamily, running a hand through her hair and bringing it all down in confusion. 'We'll walk on the strand, disturbing the curlews.'

'And a few snogging communists.'

She seemed to be looking far away into that distant land, but he was conscious of her drawing closer to him even though she had not moved from the sofa. 'We'll find a moss-green bunker,' she said in that same remote tone, 'between towering sand dunes. We'll throw off our clothes and make wild love.'

The silence was vibrant. He said, 'Really?'

'On the other hand it's a hell of a long way to go, just for that.'

'Worth every penny of the fare.'

'You can do it all in Dollis Hill any night. After the bedtime cocoa.'

'Quite.'

At last she was looking at him, asking him silent questions, smiling. 'Would you like some cocoa, David?'

'Funnily enough, I love the stuff.'

'I'll make it.'

She went back to the kitchen, and every faint clink of a mug, the snap of a switch, the sound of a drawer opening, was clear through the open door. It was music. And the music, thought David gratefully, was going to get sweeter and sweeter. Everything in his life was taking a turn for the better.

6

The tempo of work quickened gratifyingly. There seemed to be an awful lot of people in the world who owed money and an awful lot of other people who were having difficulty in getting them to pay up. Along the way, money began to come into the Manor Debt Collection Agency. It was money of a more respectable kind, King assured David Castle, than any they could ever have expected to get in that other dump. This was in a different class: really upmarket, this. David was happy to go along with the income and to start moving his books and bits and pieces into the flat, but not so sure about the philosophy. The very nature of the business, it seemed to him, was bound to involve them with people and situations which could not fail to be borderline. Also there could be something very unsettling about King's truly savage pleasure in tackling someone down on his luck in order to earn money from someone else who could afford the price of the persecution.

There was no point in discussing moral doubts with King; but David continued to have them. Of course debts ought to be paid. Commitments should be honoured. Defaulting debtors must be pursued and made to cough up. If tactful approaches failed, then regrettably a bit of pressure had to be applied. What most distressed David was the frequency with which this pressure proved necessary. He still wanted to believe that most people, faced with the truth, would be amenable to logic and sweet reason. Surely they could see when they had done wrong and give in gracefully? It was disillusioning to find that graceful surrender was rare. And the guiltier folk were, the more aggressive they got. It offended his willingness to believe in the basic goodness of all human beings.

Ronald King had never suffered from any such delusions.

Obligations had to be met, and it was usually simpler to put the boot in right away than to wait around for the sweetness and light to work.

David admitted that it was difficult to sympathize with, for example, that shiftless defaulter who had not merely been careless enough to father four children without ever earning enough to support even one, but had taken on a television set, washing machine, and dining-room and bedroom suites in the full knowledge that he would have no way of meeting the hire purchase commitments. It was impossible to condone the man's utter indifference to the fact that he was now out of a job and had few prospects of getting another, even if he bothered to look. But the thought of repossessing the lot and leaving those wailing kids in rooms stripped bare turned David's stomach. His digestion revolved again when the man's wife said, 'At least you might as well leave us the bed. The kids have pissed it often enough, it's not much use to anyone else.'

Five or six such petty incidents could sour anyone's outlook on life. And when King assured him that it would not be long before they could afford to refuse these small commissions and concentrate on the big ones, he wondered just how worthy the big ones would be.

They had a row over one middle-of-the-road case. A news-agent down the road from the office had got himself into a mess through incompetence and a misunderstanding of his legal rights rather than through deliberate negligence. David patiently explained to him how to sort out his ledger and make regular payments, and how he might ask for a stay of execution while he reorganized his accounting system. There was no expertise in his advice: he just saw that it made sense, and passed the sense of it on. King blew his top. It was not their job to help defaulters out of the mire they had got themselves into: clobbering them and collecting the fee was all that counted.

Fewer scruples were necessary when it came to dealing with unquestionable villains like Ed Becker. In place of scruples, though, you did tend to get flickers of fright in various sensitive parts of your anatomy. Becker and the Casson brothers were heavy types to get mixed up with. Also there was the danger of becoming no more than hired hands in protection rackets and underworld warfare. If the heavies couldn't collect their own loot, was it advisable for a respectable firm such as the Manor Debt Collection Agency to take on the dubious task for them? Come to think of it, was the Agency as reputable as it ought to be? David asked himself the question and then, tactfully rephrasing it, put it in a roundabout way to King.

'Five hundred up front,' was King's answer, 'and ten grand when we wrap it up for them.'

So far as King was concerned it was answer enough.

The two Casson brothers were legendary villains, and their cousin Charlie was no slouch. Now, however, Charlie was no longer part of the group. He had met an abrupt end, as might have been expected; but had not been murdered, as might equally have been expected: his death resulted from an accident on the A3 which caused him to collide with a very solid wall. It was a careless, unheroic way to go. His cousins George and Harold were very annoyed. They were even more annoyed with Ed Becker. George Casson explained it to King immediately after the funeral.

'Charlie was working for us when that articulated lorry smacked him on the Guildford bypass. He was on his way back to Bushey Mead after delivering one hundred and seventy-two grand to an associate of ours – a Mr Edward Becker.' Casson rolled the name round his mouth with something very far from relish.

'Cash?' asked King.

'Cash. But our Mr Becker claims he never received it. We know damn well he did. The day after Becker lied to us, he disappeared. He hasn't been seen since.' Casson nodded with grim politeness to a group of mourners coming down the churchyard path. 'I'm told you're a debt collector,' he went on. 'You find people and make them pay. We want you to find friend Becker.'

'Why me?'

'We're being monitored by a certain lot of CID. We're not keen on being observed in this particular recovery operation.' He held out a visiting card. 'This is our accountant. Talk to

67

him. He knows about the money, and he knows plenty more besides. Tell him I sent you.'

'My fee is fifteen per cent of everything I recover.'

'Rubbish. Find the money, we'll give you ten grand. Yes or no?'

King nodded, but ventured: 'I usually ask for a float to cover up-front expenses. Say five hundred?'

George Casson jerked his head at his brother Harold. A wad of notes left Harold's back pocket and found their way into King's.

'Where do I phone you?' King asked.

'You don't. We ring you.' As the two brothers turned away, Harold glanced back just once. 'A hundred and seventy-odd grand in cash floating around out there. Never give us reason to think that you got itchy fingers.'

King left the churchyard reverently. He could summon up a lot of piety towards a fee of ten grand.

Back at the office, he was greeted by a great deal of thumping and banging from upstairs. Something was dragged across the floor. Something fell over with a crash. King plodded up the flight and through the open door of the flat.

David Castle had apparently been trying to hang some curtains. His first attempt had brought the pelmet down over his head, and a standard lamp had suffered in the fray.

'Settling in nicely?' said King benevolently.

'I'm coping.' David swirled a length of curtain around his shoulder like a toga, and let it fall.

'Great. Quite a place. A slap of paint here, a small bar over there with a mirror and—'

'I don't want to be seen to be looking a gift horse in the mouth,' said David, 'but I've got a problem.'

'What's that?'

'There's no water.' David waved towards the kitchen annexe.

'So it's cut off. Call the water board.'

'I did. They came. There's two sinks, a bath, a boiler, and a hot and cold tank up in the roof. But none of them are connected by pipes of any description.'

68

'Crazy,' King conceded. He was in too good a mood to allow himself to be depressed by petty everyday problems. 'Get an estimate from a plumber and do the work and then we deduct it from the rent to the landlord.'

'I've got an estimate for five hundred and seventy pounds, which strangely enough I do not carry on my person.'

King studied him thoughtfully. He got the message: Castle was hoping he would offer a loan of the money. But King was still not entirely sure that the kid was going to stay with him.

At last he said, 'Okay. You need this flat, and you need running water and all the rest of it, to prove you're a substantial person – decent income, decent residence. Right?'

'All too right.'

'I've just been offered a job that'll produce ten grand. Ten thousand pounds cash. Drop your curtains for a while' – there was a thud as David did just that – 'and go out and earn your share. Which will be two grand of my ten, *if* we earn it.'

'Two grand? For me?'

'Yes.'

'What's the job?'

King outlined the story. It was plain that young Castle did not approve of any aspect of it. But he was up against it. One glance around the room and through the door at two useless taps, and his mind was made up for him.

'Desperate times,' he said, 'desperate measures.'

'Good lad. Now let's go see this accountant.'

They found Maharis at lunchtime. He was an Egyptian weighing some seventeen stone, and was obviously keen on adding to his bulk. Brushing aside any hint of a refusal, he bustled the two of them out of his hotel to a nearby Turkish restaurant and began shovelling pitta and taramasalata into his capacious mouth at a rate which King had to admire and Castle tried not to watch too closely. It was difficult to ask him questions for fifteen minutes or so – difficult, anyway, to interpret the replies as they filtered through his mouthfuls of food. At last, after some crumb-spraying generalities, King said firmly, 'It's Ed Becker we want to talk about.'

'If you rush your conversation when eating, you will suffer

considerable flatulence. I call it the Aswan wind burning across the land turning all before it into desert.'

Castle looked genuinely entranced by the poetry of it. King, remembering that curry some little while ago, decided he could do without poetic fantasies. He said, 'Where does Becker fit into the Casson empire?'

It was a classic story. A car stolen in Hampstead at six o'clock one morning would be on the cross-Channel ferry at ten and in Marseilles two days later. Within a week at most it would have reached Cyprus, a great clearing station for buyers from the Middle East. It was a good business when you had a turnover of hundreds of cars. The Cassons were in that business. 'But if you or I were to tell this to the police,' Maharis warned, 'our tongues will be cut out.'

Castle looked even less delighted than he had been by the sight of Maharis masticating.

'Ed Becker,' said Maharis, 'organizes it all for them. They give him money at the London end, he pays the thieves to steal the cars and drive them to the ferry. On the other side it is all arranged.'

'Where d'you think Becker is?'

'Disappeared. He knows Cyprus well, Middle East well, England well. He is anywhere.'

'Unmarried?' said King.

'Yes.'

'Girlfriend? He had lots of women, or a few women, or . . .'

'He had one girl I know certainly of,' said Maharis, less bombastic than he had been so far.

'And you happen to have her name and address?'

Maharis looked doubtful.

'It was George and Harold Casson sent me,' King reminded him. 'You know how they like to get things settled.'

Maharis gulped agreement. 'This Becker's girlfriend is a lady who was also seeing Charlie Casson. Fortunately for Becker, Charlie Casson died without finding that out. I can give you her address.'

King wrote it down in his notebook, and left the restaurant with Castle. Maharis stayed contentedly at the table, wolfing down Turkish Delight and coffee.

Waiting under the awning for a taxi, King was conscious of something nagging at the back of his mind. Maharis was an accountant, and had to be a good one if the Cassons chose to entrust their complicated finances to his scrutiny. But good accountants are not in the habit of giving away details about their clients or contacts. Not a spare word, as a rule. Yet at first meeting Maharis had swept the two of them round here for lunch, and talked, handing out a name and address, confiding bits of a story that did not show him or his employers in too golden and innocent a light. It was unusual. King was a bit puzzled about where it might lead.

'You go and talk to the girlfriend.' He passed the page torn from his notebook to Castle. 'Be subtle, please. And I'll be off to interview that new temp.'

'I thought she was going to be permanent?'

'She's temp until I say she's permanent. Then I'll go and check on this lorry collision that rubbed Charlie Casson out. Hope I've still got a friend who'll talk nicely to me.'

A taxi swerved into the kerb in answer to his signal. David Castle walked off in the direction of his moped.

The girlfriend, Janice Henley, was an attractive twenty-six-year-old with long legs and a wriggling, tarty walk. Her vital statistics would have presented a page three newspaper layout man with some problems; but a lot of men would have been happy to have such problems presented to them. Her voice was harsh but friendly. Even when David announced himself as a representative of the Manor Debt Collection Agency she laughed amiably, assured him she had no debts, but kept the door open and allowed him in with no great show of reluctance.

'It's about someone you might know,' he said as she stood aside for him to pass, leaning forward so that he brushed against her. 'Someone I'm making enquiries about.'

'Fancy a cup of tea?' She went into a small kitchen and he heard the rush of water into a kettle. 'Now, who's the someone you're making enquiries about?'

'A Mr Ed Becker.'

There was a moment of hush. She had stopped moving.

Then she clattered the lid of the kettle, and came back into the lounge.

'I haven't heard of that one. Becker? What's he supposed to have done?'

'It's a long story,' said David, 'and not too elevating. We believe he owes money to our clients, the Cassons.'

She ran her fingers down her hip, and plucked an invisible piece of thread from it. Her lips were very red, pouting, then parting to reveal very white, moist teeth.

'D'you know what I've been doing all morning?'

'No.'

'I've been making an erotic video. For Arabs. Well, Arab money. It all is nowadays, isn't it? Irish director, though. And what they done to me is to give me some underwear several sizes too small – so I sort of stick out more.' She twisted twice from side to side, to demonstrate the point or points she wished to make. 'If you'll excuse me a minute I'd just like to slip it all off. Okay?'

'Sure,' said David, a trifle apprehensively.

'Then we'll have a nice cup of tea.'

He was not sure whether this was a statement of fact or a sly euphemism. Only time would tell. He summoned up reserves of courage. He had come here to ask straight questions about one of her bent acquaintances. He would not allow himself to be deflected.

There was a faint pinging noise which might have been a telephone receiver being lifted; or replaced; or something else.

When she came back into the lounge she was less tautly protuberant, a bit slacker and more relaxed round the edges. And all the edges were smooth. She was carrying a video cassette. Each movement as she stooped to slot it into the video below the television set was as swinging and musical as if she had a sixteen-piece band accompanying her in the background. Janice was evidently used to moving to music.

'You'll like this.' She pressed the switch, and the screen spluttered and then glowed with colour – the colour of naked flesh. 'It's terrific, honest. It gets really hot. But I can see you're the sophisticated type. You can handle it. Mind you, this boy is really unusual.'

Her lips were parted. It was her face on the screen – when the cameraman bothered to spend a few seconds on her face – and it must all have been a paid, routine job for someone like her; yet, watching herself, she looked as eager and stunned as if she had never gone through the routine. Staggered, David had to admit to himself that the boy was indeed unusual. Quite a specimen. He must have an interesting private life – if he had the energy after his professional day.

David said earnestly, 'Look, I'm really here to see if I can find out anything about Ed Becker.'

'Becker?'

'I have an idea you do know him. That's our information, anyway.'

Janice watched her own contortions with trembling approval. Offhandedly she said, 'All right, I told you a little white lie. Of course I know Ed. But you have to be enormously discreet about people like him. You know what I mean.'

'What can you tell me about him?'

'Let's play tit for tat. I'll give you a fact. I know him, and I believe he's currently in Cyprus. Now you tell me what's this about a debt.'

'He owes the Cassons one hundred and seventy-two thousand. Or so they say.'

'The Cassons, eh?' She tried to look impressed, but somehow he felt that none of this was news to her. 'I wouldn't think Ed would want to owe the Cassons anything.'

'Apparently he does. And they're dead keen to find him.'

'I told you another little white lie,' she said silkily. 'About Ed being in Cyprus, I mean. While I was out there I phoned his mate about you. His mate says Ed will be back in half an hour, and he'll phone here. You busy for the next half hour? Or shall we hold hands and watch the movie?'

'I'm not too busy.'

The next scene on the video made him almost wish that he had found a way of opting out. The soundtrack, too, was pretty upsetting. The groans and bumps were far noisier, and the action on screen far sweatier, than anything that dismal little creep in his aikido class could ever have dreamed of.

Janice's hand was creeping through his hair. It stopped, and she withdrew it and inspected her long red fingernails. 'Your hair feels like used Brillo pads.'

'You think your friend might . . . er . . . get back early?'

'We'll have to wait and see, won't we?'

She hitched up a knee and managed to slide beside him on the arm of the chair and dexterously get the knee across his hip. Subtle she was not; but graceful, undoubtedly.

He thought of Deirdre. It ought to have taken his mind off what was going on. To some extent it did, but only at the cost of making him wonder what Deirdre would do if he tried anything like that remarkable bloke on the screen . . . and if she did that, and *he* did this, and *she* . . .

Janice said, 'You're embarrassed, aren't you?'

'Certainly not.'

'It's only human nature.'

David nodded, not trusting himself to speak.

'You're not bad-looking, you know.' Her attention had switched from her own convolutions on the screen. 'About two hundred quid would clean you up. Thirty quid on site clearance and then a decent haircut.'

He stood up. 'Doesn't look as if your friend Becker is going to ring.'

'Oh, he will. You don't have to rush off.'

'I've got work to do. I'd like to phone you later. May I?'

'They all do,' said Janice in a practised, sultry growl.

'But not Mr Becker.'

'He does,' she said. 'He will.'

David made his escape. He crossed the road, gulping in some fresh air, and had an absurd desire to give his moped an affectionate pat. He might have done so but for the fact that two men were sitting in a red Range Rover not far along the street, apparently consulting a map but looking up and obviously noting him as he reached the moped. When they caught his eye they looked away – probably making some snide remark about his appearance. David felt self-conscious and depressed. A smart flat, a smart vehicle, money in the bank, a two-piece suit just the same as everybody else's two-piece suit: was that all that life amounted to?

He shoved himself away from the kerb and puttered off round the corner, on to the main road, and off it again at the next set of traffic lights.

Three junctions later, and he was travelling along a pleasant road besides the Thames. The sun was out, and here and there were scatterings of family groups, a few couples wrapped in each other's arms, and the odd individual contemplating the river.

David became aware of a splash of colour in his mirror. It had recurred a number of times as he wove his way through the traffic. Now, with very little traffic on this riverside road, he recognized it as the Range Rover that had been waiting near Janice Henley's house.

He accelerated. There was precious little pull in the moped. The Range Rover could hold its distance just as it chose.

He hoped it was going to do just that: keep its distance.

If he could get to the next corner and swing back on to the main road through the town, he could either lose the pursuing vehicle or at least keep it snarled up in the rest of the traffic. Another two minutes and he would be able to get off this exposed road, veering closer and closer to the water's edge.

All at once the Range Rover began to overtake.

David glanced fearfully up at its bulk, shouldering nearer by the second. He tried a swift assessment of the position to his right. There was a strip of grass, a towpath, and then nothing but water.

He tried to slow down and fall back, to avoid the encroaching menace.

The Range Rover braked, and slewed suddenly across his path. David swung the moped towards the grass. A fat woman and a thin man in picnic chairs were eating buns off cardboard plates. Buns and plates were scattered as David raced between the chairs. He saw that he was running out of grass on the shallow slope, and tried to veer to one side. A heap of rubble beside a moored boat might cushion the impact. He aimed at it, and hit it with commendable neatness.

The moped stopped. David did not. To the amazement of a man who, crouched down out of sight, had been painting the boat, he was catapulted over the rubble and the cabin of the vessel into the River Thames.

As he surfaced he could hear the picnickers yelling at him. But he was in no condition to escape their wrath by swimming right across to the far bank. Doggedly he began to swim back towards the embankment where his moped lay crumpled on its side.

7

Detective Chief Inspector Caley was a cop of the old school. Finesse and smooth talking were not his line. Fifty, bullet-headed and blunt, he was the kind of man Ronald King thought he could get on with.

Taking the chair in front of the DCI's desk, he wasted no time on preamble. 'I've got a proposition to put to you. Saves waiting for you to roll up and suggest the co-operation yourself.'

'Do I know why I would want to co-operate in any way with you, Mr King?'

'The name's Ronald. And we have to talk about some sort of arrangement, don't we?'

'Financial, you mean?'

'Of course. We chat about the fact that I have my Manor Debt Collection Agency five miles from this front door and am actively seeking a partnership with one who can give me a little bit of "access" from time to time.'

Caley's thick lips parted benevolently. 'Yes, Ronald. I'd love to hear you put a price on that.'

'Pro rata I think is the phrase.'

'My business Latin is a little rusty.'

'It means payment by results. I'll be honest with you—'

'Excellent.' The smile grew broader.

'I may make five grand out of this current job. If I do, there could be one grand for you. Cash.' He waited. Caley waited, too; then almost imperceptibly nodded, encouraging him to go on. 'There was a car and lorry confrontation on the A3 just outside Guildford, September the third. An accident, apparently. I'd like to tell you some of the names involved in my enquiries and see if they ring any bells. I'm not asking for anything spectacular. Just a little light rooting around.'

Caley creaked back in his chair. 'Names?'

'The Casson brothers. Ed Becker. And an accountant called Maharis who gives me the impression of playing both ends against the middle.'

Caley stared at him disconcertingly. In spite of the un-yielding cragginess of that face there was somehow a hint that he knew more than King had thought he would. It made him uneasy. Then Caley said, 'Just a minute,' and reached for one of the phones on his desk. 'Brownlow still on the premises? Good. Ask him if he can drop in and see me before he goes. Right now, preferably.'

Replacing the phone, Caley resumed his concentrated appraisal of his visitor. He offered no explanation for the phone call, and no indication of what King might expect.

The door opened.

'That was quick. Thanks.' Caley waved the newcomer closer to the desk. 'Mr Ronald King – Detective Inspector Brownlow, Guildford CID.'

King mumbled a greeting. Two police officers in one room with him made him uneasy. He had known – from the other side – several awkward things that could be accomplished that way.

But Caley was saying amiably enough, 'Inspector, our friend Mr King has just named a few interesting names to me. As part of his duties as a recovery operative he's come across some information which he thinks might be of use to us. Right, Mr King?'

'That's right,' said King warily.

'As you yourself are an ex-detective of outstanding record' – there was no apparent hint of sarcasm – 'I believe we should take you into our complete confidence.'

'Glad to hear it.'

'Inspector Brownlow has been looking into that fatal motor car death of Charles Casson. Oh, yes, Ronald . . . Mr King. I think we got the same smell that you noticed – or is that a mistaken impression of mine?'

'I don't think your impression is mistaken.'

'It wasn't an accident,' said Caley flatly. 'Charles Casson was hammered off the road into that stone wall by a large truck. Not by accident. He was *pushed*.'

'Yes.' It came as no surprise.

'Possibly you don't see why CID have kept the lid on this?'

'Why have they?'

'Because we have a full description of the truck driver who caused the death. And we don't want to scare him away. The collision was witnessed by a lady motorist. She had the guts to follow the truck – discreetly. It had sustained a slow puncture in the collision. The driver stopped two miles up the road and got out.'

'And she got a description for you?'

'Six feet two, red hair, plaid lumber jacket, blue jeans.'

'And the truck?'

'Abandoned. Just left it there and went off.' Caley thumped the desk. 'This could get rough. You know the Casson family – round your way, Battersea. And you can see what it might add up to: a gang killing that will light a fuse.'

'Followed by a large bang,' Brownlow contributed, 'out of which CID may be able to collar another Casson or two.'

'You mentioned four names.' Caley ticked them off on his stubby fingers. 'George and Harold Casson . . . Ed Becker . . . and a man called Maharis. The first three are known to us – a lot of form. Can you tell me where we find Maharis?'

Not until I get what *I* want out of him, thought King. He hoped his face wasn't giving him away. 'No,' he lied. 'I was taken to a meet with him in a car park. Near Richmond Golf Club.' He did not much care for the way the two officers were staring at him. 'Tit for tat? You tell me why you want him particularly, and I'll go and look for him.'

Caley and Brownlow silently consulted each other. Then Caley nodded.

Brownlow said, 'The lady led us to the truck. It's registered to Kyreme Motor Parts PLC. The major shareholder is a man we can't trace – the man you met in the car park – Maharis.'

King got up. He would feel less oppressed outside, doing things his own way at his own speed.

'I'll find him,' he promised.

'Take it easy. And under no circumstances scare him off. We don't want any of them to know we're involved. Not yet.'

'They won't,' said King. 'Not yet.'

He went back to the office, hoping that David Castle would have arrived with something to report.

David had arrived. He was talking to the new temp, Miss Wilmott. King had chosen Miss Wilmott in direct contrast to the blue-rinsed hysteric they had employed for such a very short time in the old building. She was forty, frowsy, a good typist and very correct in her manner. David Castle did not seem to be making a favourable impression on her. It was not to be wondered at: his clothing was a lunatic mixture of Tyrolean gear – knickerbockers, thick socks and climbing boots.

King blinked. 'What in God's name . . .?'

'I needed a complete change,' said David defensively. 'And all I'd got handy, unpacked, was my hill-climbing gear.'

'*Why* did you need a complete change?'

He listened to the story of Janice Henley and the dip in the river, and when it was finished said, 'What's the position with the moped?'

'It'll require careful calculation whether the cost of repairs exceeds the value.'

King groaned. 'Anything exceeds the value of that mechanized abortion.'

Miss Wilmott frowned reproachfully. Such language, her eyebrows declared, was not used in the sort of business premises she had been used to.

'Perhaps you and the young gentleman would like a nice cup of tea?'

'He's neither a gentleman nor young. And he's going to be too busy to drink tea right now.'

'I am?' said David.

'Whenever you do want tea,' said Miss Wilmott with dignity, heading for the door, 'a little shout is all that is required.'

King wondered, watching her go, if he had made another mistake. He turned his mind back to important things. 'Could you drive my car on occasion, without wrecking it?' He had had the Rover for six years – an ex-Met car which he had acquired at a very good price. He loved the car. 'If you have any doubts about your ability,' he threatened, 'then say so.'

'I'm a terrific driver.'

With some apprehension King handed over a spare set of keys.

'I'm going to make another call at that hotel where Maharis hangs out. If he hasn't already flitted. While you will get back to your girlfriend.'

'I'm not due to see my solicitor,' said David pedantically, 'until—'

'I'm talking about the bumps-and-grinds expert. She obviously set you up. This time, sit on her until I tell you otherwise.'

Without waiting for any argument King took a taxi to the address where they had first encountered Maharis. Nobody was on duty behind the poky little reception desk in the hall. King went upstairs, finding an angle of the corridor from which he could look down the stair well. When a couple came out of a bedroom on the corner he touched a door knob as if just letting himself out, went downstairs but let them pass him in the hall, and then climbed the first flight again.

There was no mistaking the vast bulk of Maharis when he began to heave himself up from step to step. King backed away, let him open the door to his room, and then rushed in behind, slamming the door and forcing Maharis across the room to thud against the wall.

'How did you get here? You . . . get out . . . I call the police, I . . .'

'You gave me the name of the girlfriend.'

'I help you, and now you do this, you—'

'She got on to Becker,' said King, 'like you can get on to Becker. I don't want to do police work. I don't want some red-handed associate of yours for manslaughter. What I do want is to give the one hundred and seventy-two grand he's got back to the Cassons. Your part in this is to tell me where I find Ed Becker.'

'I can tell you nothing.'

'You can tell, or else I deliver you now to the Cassons. With a few chosen words on the subject of the way their trusted accountant has been doing sums for the other side.'

Maharis panicked. 'No, is not possible.'

'Is very probable,' said King, 'after I've duffed you over for lying to me through your teeth – which I may remove.'

Again he banged Maharis hard up against the wall; or as hard as that expanse of protective flab could be banged.

'No.' The word rushed out on a gasp of agonized breath.

'Becker's address.' King heaved again.

'He is living above pub. The Highlander, in Railton Road.'

King kept one hand on the Egyptian's shoulder. 'If you let him know I'm coming, you're going to be fat, flat, and dead. D'you understand me? D'you believe me?'

'Yes.'

'Remember it!'

King reached the Highlander a few minutes after opening time at the end of a hazy, sunny afternoon. A few youths who had been lounging outside a hamburger joint pushed themselves upright and sauntered towards the door of the public bar. Beside the saloon bar entrance was a door with the word 'Hotel' engraved in the glass panel – unobtrusive, and suggesting that it was a relic of past grandeur rather than a viable proposition today.

King opened the door and went in. A flight of stairs covered in linoleum led steeply upwards. Here there was not even a pretence of a reception desk. If it was still a hotel, it was managing without any of the trimmings.

The sun shone along a musty corridor, picking out a dull glow from a door knob. King tried the knob of one door; turned it; found the door unyielding. Downstairs a jukebox began to boom, the bass notes shaking the floor. Up here there was no other sound.

At the third attempt he found a door that opened. It was dark inside. Across the room he could just make out a faint line of light down the edge of drawn curtains. But it was not a drab, deserted room. You could smell and sense that it was in regular use. Not reaching for the light switch, King edged forwards, trying to accustom his eyes to the gloom and make the most of the pallid sunlight behind that curtain. He saw the outline of another door, opening into deeper darkness.

There was another darkness, a solid shape, suddenly between him and the door to the corridor.

'Are you King?'

King tried to fling himself to one side. A low table caught him on the kneecap, and he reeled back, off balance. The curtains were suddenly, blindingly, raked back. Light struck off a shock of red hair. The brawny six-footer wrapped an arm round King's neck and rushed him, crouching, towards the window.

'Becker, I'm telling you—'

There was nothing to tell. Glass disintegrated about his head, and he was flying . . . falling . . . crashing into a platoon of dustbins in the pub's back yard.

David had been unable to carry out King's order to sit on Janice Henley. She was simply not there to sit on. He had rung the doorbell, walked around a few times, and then settled himself in the comfort of King's Rover to keep an eye on the place until she returned. By mid-evening there was still no sign of her. If she had been pursuing her artistic career and filming during the day, perhaps she was indulging in some live theatre this evening. There was no telling when she would show up. Maybe she would be away all night with her boyfriend – Ed Becker, or whoever else might now have come into her life.

He had had enough. There was a telephone kiosk not a hundred yards away. He dialled the office number, none too hopefully. King would probably be away by now, taking it easy at home or maybe squandering some of their money in a sleazy local casino. David had already cottoned on to his partner's main weakness.

He was surprised to hear Miss Wilmott's voice at the other end. As soon as he had announced himself, she let fly: 'You just caught me going. I shall have to talk to the pair of you about overtime. Either that or you'll have to explain to Mr King about how long it takes to type out these reminder letters, and really you ought to get one of those word processors, I can tell you for a fact, Mr Castle, these letters are certainly repetitive . . .'

'Miss Wilmott, if—'

'It's not that I'm trying to earn overtime, I don't want overtime. I want it regular, nine to six. I mean—'

'Shut up,' said David.

There was a gasp. 'Mr Castle!'

'Is Mr King there,' asked David, 'or have you had any message from him?'

'No. Well, yes, in a way. I've had a message – for you, actually – not exactly from Mr King.'

'What d'you mean, not exactly from him?'

'It was passed on by the publican of some pub. That Mr King was on the way to some hospital.'

'Hospital?'

'I wrote it down. Battersea General Hospital. And something about . . .'

David hung up and made for the Rover.

He found King in a cubicle at the end of a long ward, asleep. He was not a pretty sight. There were bruises on his temple and gashes down his left cheek, and one arm was in a splint.

Pulling the curtains apart, the ward sister said, 'He fell from an upper floor. Is he a window cleaner by trade?'

Unwilling to go into the question of trade, David muttered, 'Sort of.' The sister backed away, and one of King's puffy eyes opened. 'How are you?' David asked gently.

'I'd have thought that would be obvious to a deaf, dumb, blind illiterate.'

Whatever injuries he might have sustained, King had lost none of his powers of expression.

'What's the damage?'

'Damage?' King bellowed; then bit his lip and groaned in pain. 'Damage?' he said in a lower tone. 'I'm not a Ford Transit that's been in a shunt. As to my *injuries*, there's nothing broken. However I am unable at the moment to stand upright, due to a little matter of leg ligaments being torn, strained, or sprained. Now, aren't you going to ask me how it happened?'

'How did it happen?' asked David dutifully.

'I was thrown out of a window into the back yard by that bastard Becker.'

'So you found Becker.'

'And lost him.' King explained his encounter with Maharis. 'Look, have you damaged my car yet?'

'Of course I haven't. I've been—'

'Any joy with the girlfriend?'

'Not a sign of her.'

'Then it's back to Maharis. Get to that hotel of his, don't stand for any nonsense, see if Becker's gone to report to him. If he's there, phone me and I'll let the Cassons loose on him. If he's not, then find him.'

'There's not a lot to—'

'Don't sag there like a garden gnome that's lost its fishing rod. Move. Get out!'

David got out.

A dark-skinned hotel receptionist was cleaning under his nails with a pair of scissors, tucked away in the cramped cubicle behind the counter. David crossed the hotel foyer – it took all of three steps – and said, 'I wonder if I can speak to Mr Maharis?'

'Is no one here that name.'

'How much?'

The receptionist made an exploratory gouge down the back of his thumbnail, and said into infinity, 'Ten pounds.'

David laid a fiver on the counter. It disappeared over the edge by some sleight of hand which hardly disturbed the probing motions of the scissors.

'Room 8, first floor.'

David went up the stairs fast, making sure he got to the door before there was any chance of the man phoning up with a warning. He rapped smartly on the door.

A muffled voice said, 'Yes?' Either the door was very thick, or Maharis had his mouth full again.

'Manager.'

The door opened. Maharis stared, then backed away, grabbing a wine bottle off the top of a cabinet. David moved in smoothly and hit him one aikido blow full in the chest. Maharis swayed back, drifted to one side like a punctured balloon, and collapsed.

'Look, I'm sorry,' said David. 'I'm only doing my job. And I'd rather not have to continue the programme. The next stage can get very painful.'

Maharis hauled himself up on to the edge of the couch.

'I've got a message from Mr King,' David went on. 'Unless you provide us with Ed Becker's current address, he's informing the Cassons about you. Informing them that the truck that deliberately ran Charlie off the road belongs to you. That you helped Becker steal the one hundred and seventy-two thousand.'

'What d'you want?'

'I've told you. Where do I get hold of Becker? I don't imagine he's hanging around that pub waiting for his next caller, is he?'

'How should I know?' gasped Maharis. 'Maybe he is there, maybe he has left, maybe—'

David turned the side of his hand like a knife blade, experimentally, judging the distance. 'Where?' he said very quietly.

'All right. He has a boat where he stays. It's moored at an old boatyard at Twickenham. Wardle's, Embankment Road, Twickenham.'

'I hope you're not lying to me.'

Maharis shook his head mutely. He had said all he could say for the time being. When he got all his breath back, he might start talking to someone else.

David left in a hurry.

The boatyard was not difficult to find. The evening sky was still orange with sunset, and reflections sparked in the water beyond a slipway. A couple of small boats, shrouded in tarpaulin, bobbed gently to one side. At a mooring further along the river frontage was a motor cruiser which looked more in Becker's line. David examined it cautiously from the bank, then clambered on to the deck.

The hatchway appeared to be locked. There was no sound from within; no sound anywhere apart from the gentle plop of

86

water against the hull. David studied the hatchway. His aikido skills could be summoned up to break through it, but it seemed a bit drastic until he had made quite sure this was the right place, the right vessel.

He tensed, readying himself for a decision.

It was made for him. The whole hatch suddenly erupted outwards. Six feet plus of Becker sprang through, his hair as orange as the sky and his face red with a deadly rage. David instinctively launched the blow for which he had been building up. It caught Becker a glancing blow, but enough to throw him back over the coaming and knock a gun out of his hand.

Guns were a different thing altogether. As Becker grabbed for it, David leaped off the boat and headed for the Rover. Let King put the Cassons on to this one.

As he reached the car, Becker was off the boat and on to the quay. A bullet screeched through the side window of the Rover, spraying the interior with fragments. David accelerated madly. Three more shots, and there was the twist of the wheel under his hands as one of the front tyres went. The Rover slewed to a stop. David ducked as he got out, heading for the wall of a building which offered some sort of shelter.

A wide double door opened into a dark, cluttered interior. It was some sort of boatbuilding shed, furnished with benches and paint pots and a long trestle, at the end of which wooden stairs rose through a trap door to an upper floor. David went up them fast. Hand to hand combat he was prepared to undertake. Guns he had never approved of.

In the loft were more paint pots, this time arranged with comparative neatness on long racks. In the darkness it was comforting to keep a wall of them between himself and the tall, murderous man creaking up the stairs.

'Come on out, boy, or there'll be a hole in your head.'

The place was dusty and smelt of paint, turps, varnish and any number of things to which David's nostrils promised to be allergic. He suppressed a sneeze.

'Come out *now*,' Becker was saying, 'and we'll do a deal.' He was on the other side of the rack. 'Show yourself, or you're finished.'

87

David pushed hard. The whole edifice of wooden shelving and paint cans collapsed upon Becker. David sprinted for the stairs, clutching the edge of the trap door as he went down, and closing it over his head. He groped for a bolt, and found one. It went securely home just as Becker begun to pound on the floor above.

David went out into the deepening twilight. The shadow of the building loomed above him. He waited. Something toppled over inside. Then a window higher up, near the top, squeaked open and a face, pale in the gloom, peered out.

'Mr Becker,' David called up, 'you'll break your legs if you come out that way. You'll be right alongside Mr King in hospital when the Cassons come visiting.'

'I'll make a deal.' It sounded faint and far away. 'Let me out, and we'll talk.'

'The gun.' David stepped back into the lee of the building, not caring to be strafed from above. 'Then we'll talk.'

There was a long, quivering pause. Then there was a thud, a few yards away. David took his time, making sure his eyes were correctly identifying the shape of the gun and not something else.

He then stepped out into the open. 'No money,' he shouted, 'no deal.'

'All right, all right.' The voice was not so faint this time. Becker was furious: not the type of man to surrender with good grace. 'It's in the boot of a Jag parked in the rear yard of the St George's Tavern. Now come up and let me out.'

David pondered this. 'Mr Becker, you really hurt my colleague by throwing him out of that window. He's only a debt collector. He didn't deserve that. So I'm going to let you down, as it were, by not letting you down. I'm going to feel very guilty about this,' he lamented, 'but I think of what you did to poor Mr Casson, and also to my partner, and I think you deserve what's probably coming to you.'

Becker's screams of abuse followed him as he made his way back to the Rover. Even in this uncertain light it was clear that the car's present condition would not be to Ronald King's taste. David shook his head ruefully, and once more went in search of a telephone box.

'Mr Casson? Ronald King asked me to get in touch with you.

We have Ed Becker locked in a loft at Wardle's Boatyard, Embankment Road, Twickenham. He says the money is in the boot of a Jag, in the rear yard of the St George's Tavern. I don't believe him, and I'm sure you don't either . . .'

King sat on the edge of his bed, fully dressed and ready to leave against all the advice showered on him by the doctor. He watched David Castle almost with affection as David counted out banknotes on to the blanket.

'There we are, then. Ten thousand.'

King nodded. That was what he liked about dealing with really vicious elements like the Cassons: they were totally straight. You delivered the goods, and around came a cab with the cash in it.

He noticed that David was separating a small pile of notes from the rest.

'What are you up to?'

'That's yours' – David tapped the larger pile – 'and this is mine.'

'Wait a minute, wait a minute . . .'

'Eight thousand for you, for services rendered in falling out of a window. I've deducted my two thousand commission.'

'Wait a minute,' fumed King again. 'A commission is an *ex gratia* that I donate to you – it's not something *you* deduct.'

'Comes to the same thing.'

'No, it does not. It's a matter of something called business etiquette, if you understand the meaning of that word.'

'I not only understand it, I can do better than that: I can spell it.'

They stared at each other. After an interminable moment King said bitterly, 'Okay, so now let'd have the comments.'

'On what?'

'On this Casson business. I can just hear it coming up, any minute now. I want to have all your accusations against me out and aired and dealt with, in one session. How we should never have got into it, blah, blah. All of it. Now. Then nothing more. No further rotten snideness, dressed up as superior moral judgments.'

He waited.

David said mildly, 'Maybe there's some confusion. I was pleased to do it. I need the money. Sorry.'

Delight suffused King's battered features. He could not believe his ears.

'Don't ever say sorry! Don't ever be sorry. Stick to what you've just been saying, before that. Every morning when you get up, kneel for a moment in prayer, and shout, "I need the money, I need the money!" And at last, son, you will have found something nearer than brown rice and bullshit to the true meaning of life.'

'And you owe me a hundred and seventeen pounds fifty pence estimated cost to repair my moped.'

King remained ecstatic. 'Good! Great! Wonderful! At last! You're there – we're a team. You've got it. It's all about money. Just money. You've got it.'

They beamed at each other in glowing mutual accord.

Then David said, 'Oh, just one last little thing. About the Rover . . .'

8

Indignity was something to which David Castle had been exposed more often than he cared to remember. Sometimes the austere philosophies of the martial arts had come to his aid, but they could not always be applied. You could not, for instance, very well clout a man with his hand up your crotch, asking odd questions.

'Which way does sir dress?'

David look querulously down at the little tailor's bald head.

'What does that mean?'

'On which side,' said Lennie Teitelbaum patiently, 'does sir dress?'

'Don't ask him that question again,' advised King.

'But I want to know what he means – "dress"?'

'I'll find out later,' said King to Lennie. 'I'll phone you.'

Lennie shrugged and glanced down the measurements he had been jotting on a pad. He seemed satisfied yet mildly sceptical about the results.

David glowered at Ronald King. 'I can't believe you're doing this to me. I simply can't believe it.'

'For the sake of our clients,' said King, 'and for your own sake when you finally get to court, your attire has got to be a hell of a lot different from what it is right now.'

David looked at the bolts of cloth all round the room. Each and every one of them looked appalling to him. Clothes were things you dragged on in the morning and tossed on to any convenient chair at night. They kept you warm, and so long as there was a back pocket in the jeans for a few crumpled notes, nothing further was required. He had never aspired to look like a stockbroker or a penguin.

Lennie Teitelbaum had opened out a heavy sample book

and was inviting him to look at various cloths. They came in every shade of grey – dark grey, dismal grey, and sombre grey.

'Wool worsted,' said Lennie affectionately, taking an edge between thumb and finger. 'With just a hint of your Oxford blue pinstripe. Are we an Oxbridge man, sir?'

'No, we are not.'

'You could have fooled me. You have, if I may express it this way, a certain *savoir-faire*. Now, all these' – he flipped through a number of designs – 'are summer-winter weight. Wonderfully stylish, don't you agree?'

'I have to be honest. I think they're all sort of muddy and dark.'

The tailor's obsequiousness began to give way to an offended grimace. 'I would have thought,' he said thinly, 'that they were more positive in outlook than the colour blend you're favouring at the moment, sir.' He plucked at David's jacket lapel with less affection than he had shown to his own samples. 'What might we call this – brussels sprout-green?'

'It's a primary colour,' said David with dignity. 'These bits of yours are all mixes. You can see brown hairs in that blue. I mean, that sort of opaques the colour, makes it dull and—'

'This is a trip to a tailor.' King was seething. 'We're here to order a sodding work suit. It is not the height of Paris fashion. You are unlikely to be out on the town this season with Princess Di and Charlie. This is a suit of clothes which will save you from being arrested for vagrancy.'

David rubbed his fingers across the open sample book.

'These feel itchy. I need cotton or denim on my legs.'

'Sir, the trousers will be fully lined.'

'No, I don't fancy lined trousers.'

'Am I making a suit for your friend,' Lennie appealed to King, 'or am I not?'

'He's not my friend, and you are making a suit for him.' King flipped through three cloths and pointed to a blue one with a red pinstripe. 'A suit of that material with two pairs of fully lined trousers.'

'What if I get rashes on my legs?' asked David.

'Fine. Get rashes on your legs.' King looked back at the tailor. 'When's the first fitting?'

'One week from now.'

'We'll be here.'

King was still fuming when they got outside. As the two of them trudged off down the street towards the car park, David said placatingly, 'Look, I know you're right in some ways.'

'Gracious of you.'

'I do need that rotten suit for my court appearances. So thanks for paying for it.'

'I'm not paying for it,' growled King. 'One of our clients is – though he doesn't know it yet.'

'As soon as the court case is over though, I'm not guaranteeing anything. Including that I won't hang this suit up in a cupboard, permanently.'

'With the speed of British justice, that'll be in about two years – just in time for a second suit.'

David escaped as soon as he could, to see if Deirdre had anything more soothing to offer.

Her smile helped a lot. What he really wanted was to have his arms round her again, and her mouth seeking out his and starting up that lovely little routine which was never really routine, always new. But while a smile was permissible in her office, the rest of it was not. He did not like the office, and did not like seeing her in it. It was impossible not to think of all the sadness, injustice and suffering that had flowed through the door and around the furniture, to be translated into Deirdre's income and the Jaguars and Bentleys of fat barristers.

He said, 'How soon can you get away from this dump?'

'When I've finished work.'

'I absolve you from the need to do any more on my account today.'

'I do have other clients.' It was not the best way to persuade him to be patient. She abruptly slid open a drawer in her desk. 'I got something through the post this morning. I've been sitting here wondering whether I should show it to you.'

'What is it?'

'When did you last see your son?'

'Eleven months ago. Eleven and a half.' He could almost have counted the days and hours.

'I asked their solicitor for full details of the adopter. They were very forthcoming.' Slowly she opened an envelope. 'For good measure, or just to rub dirt in your face, they've sent a photograph of your son.' As David put his hand out eagerly, she added, 'In the company of the prospective adopters.'

The husband and wife were substantial in every sense of the word: large and well fed, standing on a well ordered lawn and sporting tweed garments more expensive than Lennie Teitelbaum's range but, in David's view, equally repulsive. Sebastian looked tiny between them, but very alive, very much there. He was laughing at the camera or whoever stood behind it: Anne, in all probability.

'He's grown,' said David aloud.

He reached for a pair of scissors on the desk, and cut round the two adults, leaving a small square picture of that laughing face – a laugh trapped, frozen, gorgeous. Deirdre watched as he took out his wallet and tucked the photograph away.

'I've got to see him,' he said.

'I don't think you can. Not before the case.' As he began to get up she said, 'Shall I see you tonight? I could come round . . . if you're not doing anything else.'

He walked round the desk and touched her shoulder. It made his fingertips tingle. He said, 'Please. Do come, yes. But do remember to go to the loo first.'

'What are you talking about?'

'The water still isn't on.'

She edged her shoulder away. 'How much longer? That's really going to sound terrific in court – a four-bedroomed fully modernized flat without any water.' As he stood helplessly beside her, she said, 'Oh, I suppose you'd better come round to my place.'

She made it sound grudging; but when he got there she was working away devotedly in the kitchen, with the lids of three pans giving out a cheerful rattle, and an appetizing smell drifting through the open door.

He kissed her.

She wiped her hands on her apron and said, 'Why on earth am I doing all this for you?'

He kissed her again. 'Basic rules of hospitality. When you're my guest, I'll cook for you.'

'When do I get to be your guest? You don't even have running water.'

'The pipes will soon be in.'

'Yes? How much are they charging, by the way?'

'Nearly six hundred. That was the cheapest quote.'

'Dear God!'

'It's not my fault.'

'Not your fault that you moved into a flat with a bath, three sinks, immersion heater, hot and cold tanks, and no pipe connecting them to anything?'

'Why don't we live together and halve the expenses?' suggested David.

'You mean why don't *you* live with *me* and halve *your* expenses.'

They stared at each other; then both laughed, and he put his arms round her, and steam under one of the pan lids set up a weird whistling.

When they sat down to eat, Deirdre said, 'Business first.'

'Couldn't it wait until after?'

'After what?' When he thought it prudent not to make too blatant a reply, she went on: 'After you'd left this afternoon, I had a chat with my partner.'

David made a face and only narrowly avoided swallowing too large a mouthful. He had met the plump, self-satisfied young Hallday-Mostyn only twice, but had taken an instant dislike to him first time and reinforced the dislike on their second meeting. Hallday-Mostyn was too possessive towards Deirdre and too sneering in his dealings with anybody else.

'He's come up with an interesting aspect which may have some bearing on our case.'

David did his best to look attentive. It took some doing. He was sure there must be some good reason for Deirdre's enthusiasm, but the tale she was telling seemed wildly irrelevant to him.

In 1889, apparently, a derailed steam locomotive had plunged down an embankment near Edgware on to a public highway and demolished a certain Miss Bewick. Though unmarried, Miss Bewick was the mother of a bouncing baby girl, three years old at the time of the accident. The baby's name was Liberty. The person who had originally taken the liberty was an Irish gentleman, Mr O'Reilly, of little means. He appeared on the scene very promptly after Miss Bewick's demise, bringing a wardship case. He wanted his illegitimate child. The court noted that it suspected the real reason behind his desire for custody was that the child, as natural heir to Miss Bewick, would in due time inherit her not inconsiderable estate, cash and stocks, and four freeholds in Muswell Hill.

'Very interesting,' said David, baffled.

The interesting item, according to Hallday-Mostyn as relayed by Deirdre Aitken, was that the child had grandparents who also fought for custody. And yet the court awarded the wayward O'Reilly custody. It might have been that the grandparents were of an advanced age. The natural father went on to sue the railway company in another important ruling. The railway company refused compensation on the grounds that the runaway locomotive was not on railway property at the time: due to some obscure Act of God it was racing down the Edgware Road.

'How does this argue for my case?' asked David, way out of his depth.

Deirdre went on to explain that, according to the interpretation put upon it by her gifted colleague Mr Hallday-Mostyn, the mother of David's illegitimate child had so far removed herself from any interest in it that she might as well be as dead as the nineteenth-century Miss Bewick had been, as far as the child was concerned. David Castle was parallel with the O'Reilly character except that his principal object was not to gain cash and four freeholds in Muswell Hill.

'Mr O'Reilly fought the grandparents,' Deirdre concluded, 'who were blood relatives as close as this brother figure to whom your son's mother wishes to offer adoption. We think this could add up to some case law which gives us a real fighting chance.'

'You think that?' David did not care for the *we*.

'With this purely legal aspect we can pull it off. The rest is largely up to you. You've got to look good in court, say the right things, appear to be able to provide the right environment to bring up the child.'

'You're saying that even if the law is dead right, if I don't look prim and proper in court then we don't win?'

Deirdre laid her knife and fork across her plate. 'By the time we get to court,' she said, 'I've got to have you looking right.'

'There's my new suit,' he offered.

'New suit?'

'Thanks to Mr King—'

'When you appear in court, the less said about your Mr Ronald King, the better. Word may have got around.'

'Look, he's buying me a new suit. Isn't that something?'

'I can hardly wait to see it,' said Deirdre.

'And if I need a character witness, or some crap of that kind, in court—'

'Then we pretend we've never heard of Mr King.' Deirdre pushed the dish of potatoes towards him. 'But a character witness would certainly be desirable. Do you know anyone who has a good opinion of you?'

'Don't *you* think I have some hidden talents?'

Deirdre was clearly sorting out a choice of possible answers, and clearly deciding to drop them all.

She said, 'That Mr Hodinett you used to work for – do you think he'd come up with some favourable recommendations?'

David doubted it. But he had an excuse to visit the devious old twister. Something possibly profitable was brewing up for the Manor concern, and someone as dogged in tracking people down as Mr Hodinett unquestionably was, might be of assistance. Dangle money – or, rather, promises of money – in front of him, and he might allow himself to be wheedled into offering the odd *quid pro quo*.

The next day David went to see Mr Hodinett.

It ought to have been predictable that the dodgy, dubious Hodinett would sooner or later be tottering on the edge of senility. Nevertheless David was startled by the swift decline of his ex-employer. Cunning he was used to; woozy incomprehension was a new factor in the Hodinett persona.

'David Castle?' said Hodinett suspiciously. 'And who might David Castle be?'

'I worked for you?' David nudged, queried. 'You remember I worked for you?'

Hodinett analysed this, stooped, and reappeared with a bottle of sherry from a bottom drawer. 'Changed days, eh, Whittaker? Come to ask for your job back?'

'There's always a chance I might consider taking my job back.' David saw no objection to hedging his bets.

'Well, I and my partners will always give you the consideration of . . . I mean, the courtesy of reconsideration . . . that is to say . . . just a moment, Whittaker, I do seem to recall you did not work out your full notice . . .'

'I'm David Castle.'

'Not Whittaker?'

'No.'

'Then who the blazes is Whittaker?'

'I've no idea, Mr Hodinett.'

Hodinett took his glasses off, polished them, and renewed his scrutiny of his visitor. 'If you haven't made up your mind about wanting your job back, and you're not Whittaker, what do you want?'

'I was hoping for a character reference from you.'

Either Hodinett's glasses had steamed up again or his mind had clouded over. 'Character reference? For someone who did not serve out his notice, who indulged in strange physical jerks at the most inappropriate . . . no, Whittaker, it won't do.'

'Not Whittaker, sir. David Castle.'

'That's an improvement, anyway. But I fail to see why I should commit myself to providing a reference to a complete stranger in whatever circumstances the . . . as a matter of interest, Whittaker—'

'Castle. David Castle.'

'Castle. So be it. But why should I be expected to offer testimonials on your behalf when my recollection of you is that you—'

'I was in the office one day,' said David with great deliberation and with the volume turned up, 'and your partner Mr

Denzil showed me an article you had written for the *Historic Review*. An article on wine. Mr Denzil mentioned that you bought and sold wine and had an extensive cellar.'

'Quite a chatterbox, Mr Denzil. What's more, his mind is going. Still, there is a certain wisp of truth in what he had to say about my viticultural interests.'

'I'm trying to trace a debtor who's in the wine trade,' said David.

'Ah, we have news of an inheritance for him? Enough to lay down a rather splendid port vintage?'

'No, Mr Hodinett. *My* present employer is making inquiries. But' – David found it almost as easy to put on an ingratiating tone as it was to reach out with his right hand and despatch a victim over his left shoulder – 'we did feel that a real expert, a true professional within the trade, might be able to save us a great deal of time. For suitable remuneration, of course.'

'Ah,' said Mr Hodinett, beginning to wake up.

'Possibly your contacts are not quite wide enough to—'

'I can give you quite a few introductions,' said Mr Hodinett, bristling.

'Exactly what we need. I'm sure your co-operation will be invaluable. Before we get down to the details, though' – David produced his most winning smile – 'may I count on your character reference?'

'I've never had anything but the highest regard for you,' said Mr Hodinett. 'Has anybody ever said otherwise?'

9

Rodney Finch-Courteney was in his late thirties and could continue to pass for that in a nightclub or intimately lit restaurant. In a good light – that is, daylight – he looked a ravaged fifty. It was daylight now, and the setting did little to help. Finch-Courteney never actually said 'Eton and the Guards' when introducing himself, but did manage to convey awareness of the pedigree. He looked very out of place today, parked in a schoolyard and hiring a trestle table on which to lay out the contents of his car boot. Most of the items were personal belongings: even if he had had any of it available, his old stock in trade would have appeared just as incongruous here as he himself did.

Finch-Courteney had been in the wine trade. His one-man firm had won the plaudits of the wine correspondents and attracted the money of connoisseurs and impressionable impulse buyers. Many people were easily impressed by fine labels and fine phrases; and Rodney at his suave best could be equally impressive. Now he was bankrupt.

It had been good while it lasted. Perhaps it could have gone on being good if he had not been so greedy. It had worked very well for a while, along classic, acceptable lines. Take a great vintage like the Bordeaux of 1982; one knew in advance there would be a lot of people anxious to buy *en primeur*, when the wine was still maturing in the vats at the chateau. By the time it was bottled and in the hands of the merchants, the price would have gone through the roof. Finch-Courteney, with valuable contacts at some of the most admired chateaux, knew what to reserve and when. Then he would send out his list, and back would come the cheques. For several years it worked predictably and rewardingly. Then came the huge publicity about that major vintage, and the cheques cascaded in. He had never seen so much money – a vast outlay, money paid in full by customers for wine which they had not got. It was not just the blindly eager customers who had no wine for the time being: Rodney Finch-Courteney himself did not have those reserves. Money kept coming in for claret he could not hope to supply.

Somewhere at the back of his mind maybe there was an idea that he would use the money to make a few killings at the race track and in the City. Make some quick profit, and then when the year or eighteen months had passed and the time came to deliver the goods, he would return the money with apologies. It was a bit like a bank, really: he had the use of the money, he invested it wisely, and nobody was much the worse when he wound the whole thing up.

Only it had not worked out that way.

A dispassionate critic might have made snide remarks about Finch-Courteney's old school chums in the stock market who had let him down and then given up answering his phone calls. It was easy to envisage them passing by on the other side of the railings and quickening their pace as they saw pathetic old Rodney heaving his television set out of the Granada on to the trestle and arranging cutlery, an electric toaster, and an elegant silk dressing gown around it.

A Rover 3500 was waved by one of the marshals into a slot alongside the Granada. Around the yard a number of hatchbacks were disgorging miscellaneous junk, all to be stacked up in some sort of order before the public streamed in at three o'clock. Only the two men in the Rover, tipped off in a roundabout, confused, but ultimately intelligible mish-mash of suggestions by Mr Hodinett, were not yet getting out.

A marshal tapped on the driver's window. 'If you'd like a trestle table, that'll be one pound extra.'

'Yes,' said David Castle.

'No,' said Ronald King.

'Which is it?'

'It's no.'

'Yes.'

As the marshal strode disapprovingly away, David said, 'We

have to manoeuvre into a position where we can approach him. If we're fiddling about with a trestle table like everybody else, it looks less suspicious.'

'What is this – method acting?' King glanced across at Finch-Courteney, and glanced quickly away. 'Don't look at him. Just keep talking. Come on, I usually can't stop you.'

'Well ... er ... d'you think anxiety dreams necessarily mean one is going through an anxious psychological period?'

'What the hell does that mean?'

'All last week, each night, I dreamt I was playing Ivan Lendl. Each night it went to five sets. Every game a total humiliation, ending in my total collapse.'

'That's why you look like a ghost – up all night, playing tennis.'

'Now I'm worried. I haven't had the dream for three nights. Now if I have to play him tonight, I'll be out of practice.'

King opened his door. It looked as if a bit of trading was already going on before the general public could get near. A man from another parked car had sauntered over and was pointing at the television set. Whatever price Finch-Courteney was asking, it was clearly too high. The potential buyer shrugged and went back to his own table. King and Castle edged around, looking at the junk behind a decrepit station wagon which could only have won its MOT by bribery and corruption. King nodded at a particularly loud checked jacket.

'May I remind you to collect your suit from my tailor at the earliest possible opportunity?'

'And may I remind you that there are conditions attached? I will not wear a suit or uniform if it is unwearable. I am not into suits.'

'Really. So what are you into?'

David was showing intense interest in a soap rack. 'I think our friend has clocked us.'

It had always been a risk. King acknowledged that the man could have noticed them when the Rover pulled in behind at the traffic lights half a mile back. Finch-Courteney was liable to get a permanent crick in his neck from all those years of looking over his shoulder.

He said quietly, 'We go slowly back to the motor. We appear to head round the boot. You get in the left side, I get in the right. Then we'll play it as it lays.'

'Play what as it lays?'

King decided to ignore this. He led the way round the back of the Rover. Their quarry was definitely watching them by now. He made a cautious move round his own vehicle, but found himself on the passenger side. King closed in. With a sudden thrust Finch-Courteney dived across the passenger seat towards the driver's seat. David Castle was there before him. As Finch-Courteney lashed out, David grappled with him and tried to hold him steady. Nails clawed down his face. David winced, and delivered one skilful jab to that pallid forehead. Finch-Courteney screamed.

King was leaning in. 'If you don't want any more pain, get in my motor. Come on, Rodney.'

'Who are you?'

King raised a threatening fist. David gave a shove from behind. Finch-Courteney lurched across the gap between the two cars as a marshal and a couple of other dealers came curiously over the playground.

'Domestic trouble,' said King loudly. 'Family row. They're brothers. This one's walked off with the family silver.' He opened the back door of the Rover and ushered the other two in.

'Where are you taking me?' whined Finch-Courteney as King got into the driver's seat and flicked the ignition.

'To meet an employee of Mr Devas.'

Rodney Finch-Courteney moaned. One of the marshals shouted. But the Rover slewed round, skidded, and raced back down the lines of cars, past another wide-eyed marshal and out on to the road.

Nothing was said for a few minutes, then Finch-Courteney summoned up the strength to complain. 'You know this is technically kidnapping.'

'No, it isn't,' said King. 'We're escorting you to a meeting with your creditors.'

'Maybe he has a point,' David mused. 'It must be some kind

of technical abduction. But you see' – he turned with grave reasonableness to their cowering passenger – 'you have committed an act that must be defined as a fraud, so technically we could restrain you in the sense that technically we're entitled to make a citizen's arrest. Which means in law, I'd think, that we have the power technically to restrain. Now, whether that power to restrain—'

'Why don't you technically shut up?' said King over his shoulder.

He turned into a long crescent, and then under an arch to a cobbled mews. They bumped to a halt. Approaching from the other end was a chauffeur-driven Jaguar. It stopped facing the Rover, and a tall, fair-haired man in a sleekly tailored lightweight suit got out. King would have liked to draw David's attention to the cut of that suit, but they had other things on their mind right now.

Rodney Finch-Courteney certainly had something on his mind. At the sight of the man approaching he let out a little whisper of fear.

King wound down his window.

The newcomer said offhandedly, 'Come.' He opened the front door of the mews house outside which they had stopped. King and Castle chaperoned their victim to the door and through it, on into a sitting room whose carpet breathed opulence.

Finch-Courteney hardly seemed to be breathing at all.

'I am Peter Jansen Mowbray, PPS to Mr Devas.' The fair-haired man introduced himself to King, sparing David Castle no more than a fastidious glance. He opened a black briefcase with a gold monogram on its side and said, much more coldly, to Finch-Courteney, 'I have some documents for you to sign. Now, if you'll excuse me just a moment . . .'

He went into the next room. The three of them, silent, heard an intermittent murmur which was obviously one end of a telephone conversation. Even unable to pick out a word of it, Finch-Courteney grew paler and more tremulous. All news today was bad, and getting worse.

When Mowbray came back he addressed King again: 'Mr

Devas instructs me that your brief is now to include keeping our friend here in this house today and tomorrow, and till bank opening time on Monday.'

King had not bargained for this. He had been hoping to hand over the prey, collect the fee, and relax for the rest of the weekend.

Rodney Finch-Courteney protested: 'I'm not staying here.'

'You are most decidedly staying here,' said Mowbray. 'You are staying put and doing, from now on, exactly as you're told. And Mr King . . . the fee for keeping this chap under wraps until Monday will be extra to our original arrangement of ten per cent of everything you recover.'

'Right.' King perked up. 'Can be done.'

Mowbray produced two sets of keys and handed them both to King. King passed one set on to David. Mowbray viewed this with mild concern, but made no comment. He switched his attention to the hapless Finch-Courteney again. 'Mr Devas is flying in from Geneva this afternoon. I'll confirm the details for Monday after I've spoken to him. Meanwhile let's get the documentation out of the way, shall we?'

'I'm not signing anything.'

Aloof and implacable, Mowbray took a folder from the briefcase, opened it out to display two typed pages, and laid a gold pen across the foot.

'From our records,' he said, 'we have confirmed paying money into two of your bank accounts. These pro forma letters request your bank to surrender me statements of both accounts.'

'Nothing there. Nothing in either of them.'

'We'd rather the bank tells us that on Monday. Put the numbers of the accounts, and your signature there . . . and there.' Mowbray picked up the pen and held it out. Rodney Finch-Courteney hesitated, looked wanly into Mowbray's face, and then leaned over the sheets and wrote. 'There's a story, you know,' observed Mowbray with apparent dreamy irrelevance, 'that when Mr Devas was in shipping and somebody let him down badly, he revived the noble old tradition of keelhauling. When the misguided miscreant came out of the water, he had no skin on him – anywhere.' He put the pages back into his briefcase. 'Right, Mr King? I can leave you to cope?'

'Nothing here we can't handle.'

It was not until they had heard the Jaguar's engine echo gently away down the narrow, resonant mews, that David said, 'I want to talk to you.'

King gestured Rodney to sit down and stay sitting. He spread his hands, waiting. David took one arm and steered him to the far side of the room.

'So this is what you've got us into,' he said in a passionate undertone. 'A client who keelhauls his debtors. "No skin – anywhere." Very pretty, isn't it?'

'Piece of reported anecdote. Nothing more.'

'This is highly illegal. We can't hold this man here all over the weekend.'

'Quite right. Doesn't take both of us. You can do it single-handed.'

'No.'

'You want to resign?'

'I've made definite arrangements to see Deirdre this weekend.'

'Invite her here,' said King expansively. 'Nice plushy surroundings. I'm sure Rodney would turn a blind eye.'

'*She* wouldn't. She'd soon be on to how illegal this is.'

King sighed. 'All right. You do today, I'll do tomorrow. Fair?' Before David could dredge up any more puritanical arguments, King handed over a fiver. 'There's a shop just round the corner. Purchase a packet of tea bags, milk, a pound of sugar. Oh – and some sardines.'

With a sullen lower lip David went off on his errand. King watched from the window to make sure he was well and truly on his way, and then turned towards their captive. Rodney was sitting at the table with his head in his hands. King was not sure that the proprietor of this plushy establishment would want elbows of that kind greasing up his table. With one deft movement he wrenched Rodney up on to his feet, got his left arm in a half-nelson, and snapped handcuffs out of his pocket on to Rodney's right wrist.

'What are you doing?'

King marched him off into the small but lavishly appointed kitchen. He shouldered Rodney close to the sink unit and snapped the other end of the handcuffs round the tap fitment.

'I can't believe you got rid of all that money. A few horses, a hell of a lot of piss-ups with your ex-Etonian yobbos, all right. But not *that* much.'

'Why do you suppose I was endeavouring to dispose of my personal property at that—'

'Ready cash can be difficult. Okay. But somewhere you've got some assets neatly tied up. I'm going to fine-toothcomb your residence. There's a dodgy glint in your eye, Rodney old lad, and I can't put it all down to your being an ex-public-schoolboy.'

Rodney rattled his handcuffs against the tap. 'Take these things off! Let me go, and we could talk, maybe we could . . .'

King was already on his way out into the mews and into the Rover.

Rodney Finch-Courteney's flat above Eccleston Square ought to have been representative of the upwardly mobile society. A few years ago it had conceivably been just that. Now, in spite of being on the first floor, it had a fusty atmosphere of what could only be described as rapidly escalating downward mobility. Without knowing categorically that the rent had not been paid for quite some time, and without knowing what shifty evasions the tenant might have contrived, King sensed in his bones the creak of financial rheumatism.

There was a framed photograph of Rodney himself on an occasional table. King had never considered framing a photograph of himself, let alone introducing it into his immediate surroundings. On one wall was a dark space from which a painting had been removed. Maybe it had been in the boot of the Granada, awaiting the moment for a sale in that school playground; or maybe it had been more profitably disposed of before the ultimate degradation.

Still King could not quite accept the speed of that collapse. Shortage of ready cash, yes; desperation to get beyond the reach of Devas and his cohorts, yes; but not the utter disappearance of all that carefully laundered money which Finch-Courteney had drawn into his maw.

He opened the drawer of a slender little table which would surely have fetched a little bit of cash. The drawer was empty, and its bottom proved to be of slightly warped plywood. Not quite what it seemed. Like its owner, thought King – and then twitched with the thought that he was in danger of getting notions as critical as those of David Castle.

He tried the toilet. On a ledge beside the lavatory pan was a mixture of copies of *Playboy*, *Country Life*, and the *Economist*. He lifted the porcelain top off the slim-line tank behind the seat. A black ledger had been tucked away there, inside a plastic bag.

It looked promising. King opened out the ledger, and noted some names, addresses and prices.

Strictly speaking he ought to have been prepared to honour his promise and relieve David in the mews premises. But it would do young David no harm to learn who was boss. King now knew what the next stage was, and wasting a whole Sunday had nothing to do with it.

First thing on Monday morning he was in the wine store in Battersea, opening up the black ledger and intimating that the manager ought to be able to come up with some answers.

'Purchased and paid for?' he challenged.

The manager, a trim little man with, in all probability, no palate but a very good computer and a book-keeper who had been with a rather better firm before some peccadillo had reduced him to seeking employment elsewhere, said, 'It's certainly paid for, minus a couple of quid a case duty, plus freight charges.'

'From these pages can you give me the roughest idea of what the lot might be worth?'

The manager ran his gaze over his entries. 'Well, a lesser growth claret, but a respected one. Let's say sixty quid a case.' He made a quick assessment of the quantities. 'Twelve cases is seven hundred and twenty pounds plus your retail profit at ten to thirty per cent. Say nine hundred pounds.'

The pace was quickening. King felt well tuned up for the meeting with Mr Devas and his entourage that same Monday afternoon. He collected Rodney and David – ignoring David's resentful queries about how the hell he had spent his Sunday, and some sarcastic additions about whether he had gone to church or made do with *Songs of Praise* on the telly.

City and Central Properties occupied two floors of a glass-and-concrete tower overlooking the Thames. The chairman's office had a long, deep window offering a gleaming view across the water to the uneven skyline of south London. Devas seemed unconcerned with the view; or maybe he had already had his fill of it. He sat with his back to the window, reading a company report and paying no attention as Jansen Mowbray ushered his visitors in. The three men lined up in front of the desk, King and Castle standing to either side of the sagging Rodney Finch-Courteney.

When at last Devas looked up, Rodney burst out, 'I must protest at my treatment! Abducted, chained, literally chained . . .'

'I don't want to hear you say anything.' Devas spoke in a deep, cultured drawl which just failed to disguise a deeper East European accent. 'There is nothing left for you to say.' He tossed the report aside and crouched forward. 'For twenty years I've used little negotiants like you, each one as scrupulous as the next in their dealings. Then Lord Densey recommends you. Later it turns out that he's never once purchased wine from you, and recommended you only because you're old school chums. Well, you're not an old school chum of mine.'

'It was all an unfortunate misunderstanding,' bleated Rodney.

'I'll agree that you failed to understand me or my expectations.'

'I'll do what I can to make amends. Given time—'

'Time?' Devas smiled a thin, menacing smile. 'You might very well expect to be given that. But I don't think sending a chap like you to jail is enough. That's why you're here. I have a number of tasks in mind for you. Starting right away, actually.' He looked coolly at King. 'If you and your associate would kindly withdraw for a moment.'

Mowbray opened a door into an ante-room. A blonde secretary was typing in one corner. David shifted his weight from one foot to another. King looked about the room. It spoke of money, which was a language he approved of. Some of it was due to come his way very shortly, when he had wrapped up the last aspects of the deal with Devas.

Mowbray had gone back into the inner sanctum. He was not there long. When he returned, Rodney Finch-Courteney was cowering beside him.

'You will collect our friend's travelling requisites from his home,' said Mowbray curtly. 'Don't let it take more than five minutes. Then drop him at Heathrow, come back and see me, and I'll settle your account.'

This was not quite how King had pictured it. 'But what about the wine?'

'Please go. Mr Devas would not wish him to miss his plane.'

Mowbray waved a dismissive hand, and was gone. David looked a silent, puzzled question at King. Just as puzzled, and nagged by the apprehension that the wine part of the deal was somehow slipping away, King grabbed Rodney's arm and steered him out of the room towards the lifts.

'Why are we going to the airport?' asked David, as they got into the Rover.

King accelerated away fast. 'Ask him, not me.'

'Well?' said David to Rodney.

'None of your business.'

King braked fiercely and screeched to a halt beside the kerb. Somebody blazed a furious horn at him. He swung round, yelling across the back of the seat at Rodney.

'You are very much my business. I was down to make a nice return of ten per cent of all wine recovered. Now you come out of a huddle with those two and it's all airports and "settle the account" and now nobody's talking about wine.'

'There is no wine,' said Rodney sullenly.

'There bloody is.' King stooped and dragged the black ledger out from under his seat. 'And the reason I didn't tell Mr Devas about this is I think there's more, you thieving little rat. And when you come back from this mysterious journey, you and I will be going into a dark alley and you'll be telling me where the rest of the stuff you nicked is.'

'You don't frighten me. You know why? Because compared to Devas you're nothing. Nothing at all. All he has to do is pick up a phone, and I'm on my way to South Africa.'

'What for?' David demanded.

'I have to fly to Belgrade.' Rodney was beginning, perversely, to revel in his own importance. 'Then to Cairo, pick up a package, and fly to Johannesburg.'

'What package?'

'Oh, he's quite open about it.' Rodney's self-confidence was growing by the second. 'It's a gun sight. A night sight for a gun. Something very special for the South Africans to copy. He says the British Government are very difficult about these things.'

David was outraged. 'A gun sight!' he breathed. 'Are you listening to this?'

King shrugged. A part of a gun was a part of a gun. But he might have guessed, of course, that young Castle would have been anti-apartheid and all the rest of it.

'Aiding in sanctions busting,' David was ranting on. 'Helping a Fascist regime . . . breaking British law . . .!'

King kept his eyes on Rodney Finch-Courteney, whose confidence ebbed away as fast as it had come. 'You could be in a lot of trouble,' said King levelly. 'Big international trouble – tougher than you can imagine. I can offer you a simple way out of it. Stop lying about the wine. Give us sixty pounds' worth to give back to Mr Devas and we won't take you to the airport.'

Rodney reacted with unexpected speed. He suddenly swung round on David and threw a wild punch. It landed on David's nose, bringing tears to his eyes and a howl to his lips. The door was thrown open. Rodney fell out, stumbled, and then was away.

'Get him!' bellowed King.

Clutching his bloodied nose, David lurched out on to the pavement. But Rodney was quite a sprinter when he had to be. He was a good hundred yards ahead before David could force himself to see straight, and in a matter of seconds was round a corner and into a network of side streets and alleys.

They had lost him.

King did not relish the prospect of reporting to Devas in person. When they had got back to the office he took a swig of whisky out of the bottle in the top of his filing cabinet, and with great effort picked up the phone.

Peter Jansen Mowbray was not pleased when he received the news. He would report to Mr Devas and then ring back; and Mr King would please not move away from the telephone until that call was made. When he did ring back, it was to say that Mr Devas, too, was not pleased. Mr Devas was in fact very disappointed.

King had one card to play. It was time to produce that ledger. Perhaps Mr Mowbray would be good enough to notify Mr Devas of the good news – after all, the wine was what had really been behind it from the start, wasn't it? – and they could have a chat and sort everything out.

Yes, tomorrow morning would suit nicely.

Mowbray relieved King of the ledger the moment he arrived; and then he and his high hopes were kept waiting a good twenty minutes while Devas presumably condescended to give his attention to the entries.

At last King was summoned into the presence.

'Sit down, Mr King.'

King sat.

'I'm very disappointed that you let our friend go.' Devas sat back in his chair and gave his visitor a long, disconcertingly chilly look. 'Incompetence always distresses me.' He allowed another long pause, then said, 'As to this ledger, I've studied the contents, and if this is the kind of wine Rodney has salted away I'm not interested. It's all rather inferior stuff.'

'Oh, I wouldn't say that.'

'*I* would,' said Devas crushingly. 'Now, I want Rodney back and sent on a commission we arranged for him. As you have been so very far from efficient in your handling of the matter so far, I'm putting others on to the task. Mr Jansen Mowbray will settle your account, with deductions for negligence. So our business appears to be at an end.' He handed the ledger across the desk.

King said, 'What about my percentage?'

'Of what?'

'Of the value of the wine recovered. Once I've got my hands on it—'

'Goodbye, Mr King.' Devas produced one of his least endearing smiles, and pressed a buzzer on the desk.

10

David had been wrestling with his conscience. The conscience showed every sign of coming out the winner, immune to his most devious aikido tactics. In the end he mentally offered the ritual genuflection of defeat. Settling himself at his desk he found, after some discreet telephoning, that the correct authority to notify about illegal shipments of gun sights and suchlike was the Minister of State at the Foreign Office. Rather than trust Miss Wilmott with such sensitive material he began to draft a suitable letter himself, establishing his main characters and basic situation without revealing too much about the procedures and professional ethics of The Manor Debt Collection Agency. The more concise the communication, the better.

> Mr Rodney Finch-Courteney was approached recently by Mr Devas of City and Central Properties and requested to smuggle a gun sight, or a gun night sight, into South Africa. I am prepared to swear on oath that this was told to me by Mr Finch-Courteney, who can be contacted through me.

He paused before adding the 'Yours faithfully' and the signature. That concluding promise was a pretty thin one. They had failed to stop Rodney slithering through their grasp once already. What chance did they have of finding him again, grabbing him again, and this time holding on more firmly?

It was a doubt abruptly and unexpectedly swept away. The door was thrust open by King's left elbow. His right arm held Finch-Courteney's in a tight lock as he marched him into the room.

David gaped up admiringly. 'You found him!'

'Of course I found him.'

King flung Rodney into a chair and was about to close the door when Miss Wilmott put her head round it. 'Would your visitor like a cup of tea?'

'If he would,' said King, 'he's not going to get one.'

Miss Wilmott withdrew, hurt.

David said, 'How did you get to him?'

'Me, I don't like to be hired to do something and then be told to forget it. I wanted our Rodney here, and I want every bottle of wine he's stashed away against his old age. I'm going to recover ten per cent of the value of it.'

Rodney said, 'You heard Mr Devas, he's no longer interested—'

'He'll be interested enough if he finds you did buy his wine after all and hid it away, and I track it down for him.' King perched on the edge of the desk, holding forth smugly to David but not taking his eyes off their captive, who was going to stay captive this time. 'Did you know our friend here trades under another name? My old mate Bernie put me on to that. A bit lower end of the market, Bernie, but he knows the *class* when he sees it. *Class*,' repeated King wryly. 'Anyway, he passed me on to another gentleman a bit higher up the ladder who's been looking for him for some weeks, because naughty Rodney hasn't been paying the rent on a large lockup. Only it wasn't Rodney on this occasion. Let me introduce Roger Vane Hailsbury. No wonder there was some difficulty trying to trace all those lovely bottles. But I found the lockup – and then I followed my nose and found Rodney. Can't get used to calling him Roger yet.'

Rodney attempted: 'You've no right to drag me here. And you're not going to drag me back to Mr Devas again. I shall call the police.'

'Unlikely. Several ways you can accompany me to Devas's office. One way is with broken teeth. And once we've handed you over, I go after some more wine. I scent several thousand quids' worth nestling in some cellars. A few dockets I picked up from that little cache' – he tossed them on the desk in front of David – 'so just you sit down with our friend and see if you can find out anything else that's going on. Meantime I'm going to have a word with the Lord of Devas.'

King strode off complacently to his own office.

David gave Rodney a reproachful shake of the head. 'It seems you've been lying again.' He turned over the dockets. 'Any more where these came from?'

'That's all I have left, I swear it. And none of it would interest a real expert. Really.'

'So you're going to have to fly off at Devas's bidding after all.' David fished out his draft letter, altered two words in the first line, pursed his lips with satisfaction over the fact that there was no need to modify the final paragraph, and then read it out loud. 'All right?' he said, when he had concluded.

Rodney stared, stupefied. 'Are you stark, staring . . .'

King was back. 'Right. Let's toddle along, Mr Finch-Courteney or whatever. Mr Devas is waiting.' He nodded to David, and the two of them flanked Rodney as he slunk out towards the car. This time he made no attempt to escape. He seemed stunned, sunk in on his own thoughts. The only movement he made as they drove along was to turn his head and look wonderingly at David.

The office was exactly the same as it had been before. Devas was behind his desk, Jansen Mowbray was languidly draped over an armchair. This time, though, Devas was positively courteous.

'Well done, Mr King. So glad you found him. I feel disposed to offer an extra fee. Shall we say a thousand?'

'Thank you,' said King with matching courtesy.

'You'll have a cheque tomorrow. Now I think that does conclude our business.' David half expected King to make some statement about the wine, but evidently he was intending to play this one close to his chest. Devas rose to his feet, Jansen Mowbray was uncurling himself to escort them to the door. 'Goodbye, Mr King. And . . .' He glanced at David but decided not to pursue the matter. As they reached the door he was already turning his attention to Rodney. 'Now, can I assume you've got over your fit of nerves and you're ready to undertake that little trip? You really should encounter no problems.'

Jansen Mowbray held the door open. The last words David heard were Rodney's blurred, stumbling, 'Problems? . . . I tell you, there's a problem . . .'

The door closed behind them.

On the way out, King said, 'I'm going to sniff around a few vaults before our friend gets back from wherever he ultimately lands. You get back to the office and see what's in the second post. Ought to be a few cheques. And maybe something about that money-lender and the two gays he fancies—'

'Fancies?'

'If you'd let me finish, I was about to say fancies lowering the boom on.'

David made his way back to the office, stopping only to pick up some sandwiches and an apple for a makeshift lunch.

Miss Wilmott greeted him with an arch smile of which he would not have thought her capable. 'There's a young lady waiting for you upstairs, Mr Castle.'

'Why didn't you show her into the office, give her a cup of tea?'

'She said it was . . . personal.' The word reverberated with a number of throbbing undertones.

David went up to his flat. Deirdre was sitting at the table, scribbling a note. When she looked up and saw him, she tore the note across and tossed it towards a rusty tin which served as a waste-paper basket. She missed.

'I've just brought your clean laundry back. Thought I'd drop it in as I was driving past this way.'

'Thanks.' He leaned over and kissed her.

'I see the water's on at last.'

'That's right. Everything working.'

'So you can do your own washing from now on.' She got up and reached for her briefcase.

'It won't be the same.'

'For me it certainly won't,' said Deirdre happily.

'Don't rush off. I can actually offer you a cup of coffee now. Then we could . . . well, rumple a few sheets and then I'll test the—'

'David, I have to be in court in an hour.'

'They can wait. Do 'em good. Parasites.'

'You won't want to be kept waiting when *your* turn comes.'

He waited until she was at the door, then slid up behind and put his arms around her. She had a slim but far from bony waist: warm, soft, reluctant to escape from him. And there was a lovely smell in the nape of her neck.

David said, 'Come here for dinner this evening? With a packet soup and running water, I can work wonders.'

She hesitated. 'I ought to be reading up on some—'

'Just a drink. A bowl of soup. And anything else that takes your fancy and won't last too long.'

'I hate rushing things.'

'But you're rushing off now.'

'Thanks for reminding me.'

He went downstairs behind her, closed the outer door, and wandered without much enthusiasm into the office.

Miss Wilmott was on the phone. As he came closer she put a hand over the mouthpiece and said, 'Has Mr King been ordering some wine?'

'Wine?' David woke up from the last wisps of daydreams about Deirdre. 'Here, let me take that.' Into the phone he said, 'David Castle here.'

'Bernie Breck. Thought Mr King might be about.'

'I'm his . . . associate. We're working on a wine case together.' The moment he had said it, he wanted to laugh; but the man at the other end of the line did not have the same sense of humour.

'Ronnie King was round here first thing this morning, asking me about a Rodney Finch-Courteney, only it turned out he was operating as Roger Vane Hailsbury, and—'

'That's all right, Mr Breck. Thanks for ringing, but we did manage to find him. I fancy he'll be on his way out of the country this afternoon.'

'Oh. That so?' Bernie Breck sounded baffled. 'Well, I suppose you know what . . . I mean, it's just that I've just this minute had a tip-off from my cousin Edwin that Rodney or Roger has just been round Hadley's Wine Auctions.'

'Just been round . . .?'

'Not ten minutes ago. Jimmy Bartlett-Page – you know, top boy there – had a visit. Rodney wants to deliver a big bunch of '82s for Thursday week's auction. Said he'd be back at Hadley's in about half an hour.'

'Where is this place?'

'Hadley's Wine Auctions, Tooley Street.'

David put the phone down and reached for the petty cash box to find some taxi fare. Miss Wilmott protested – 'Mr Castle, I do have to keep a record of every ingoing and outgoing, you really mustn't rummage like that, I'll never keep the books straight' – but he was already on his way out.

The wine warehouse was a tall, grim building with barred windows and great iron bolts on its large green doors. The only indication that its contents offered pleasure rather than punishment was a noticeboard announcing weekly wine auctions. David stationed himself in a shop doorway across the street, half concealed by a rack of newspapers.

He had arrived just in time. Before he had had a chance to skim the headlines of more than two newspapers on the rack, a Ford Transit came up the street with Rodney at the wheel. He looked determined as he stopped and hurriedly he got out. He quickly opened the rear doors of the van to reveal a pile of wooden wine cases. David crossed the road and stood at his shoulder.

'Where you taking this wine, Rodney?'

Finch-Courteney put out a hand to steady himself against one of the open doors, then spun round. 'What the hell d'you want? Mind your own damn business.'

'Why aren't you on that plane, Rodney? Why are you in such a tearing hurry?'

'I've told you once—'

'Does Mr Devas know you're filling time in like this? It's not your wine, Rodney,' David emphasized. 'So it can't go into a wine auction.'

'I put the money down, so I can sell it. I paid for it—'

'But not with your own money. Now, either I get the police or I get into this van and we drive it off for a little more detailed investigation. What's your decision, Rodney?'

'I want to get rid of this and get out,' moaned Rodney. 'That's all. Just get out of my way, let me unload . . . I mean, look, in your own way you seem quite a decent sort. I don't know what school you went to, old chap, but you're a credit to it, and don't say I'm not the first to acknowledge that—'

'Why aren't you on that plane, Rodney?'

'Plans were changed.'

'Why were they changed?'

'After I'd told Mr Devas about that lunatic letter of yours—'

'You told Devas?'

'You didn't tell me not to,' said Rodney with all the plaintiveness of a misjudged schoolboy.

'Come along, Rodney.' David's authoritative calm disguised – or, at least, he hoped it did – his flicker of alarm about the possible consequences of Devas having been alerted to the danger of that letter. 'We'd better sort everything out back at the office. A few comparisons of dockets and crates, don't you think? And some questions about what's still missing.' He slammed the Transit's doors shut, and waved Rodney towards the driving seat.

As they set off, Rodney grew even more plaintive. 'You don't know what a mess you're getting into. *And* getting me into. It's persecution, that's what it is: persecution.'

'Just tell us about all the other wine you've got,' said David soothingly, 'produce the invoices, and then we might offer some assistance in clearing up this mess for you.'

Rodney Finch-Courteney slumped back in his seat, narrowly missed a bus coming round the corner, and then concentrated on the road.

'Left here,' said David. 'Take it easy. Wouldn't want to knock the one-way street sign over, would we? Right at the bottom of the hill, then slow down for a left again. And then we're there.'

He was surprised to see a 'Closed' notice dangling in the office doorway. King ought surely to have been back by now. Certainly his researches could not have led him to Rodney, for Rodney was right here. David eased himself out of the Transit; and then spotted that the front door to the ground floor hallway of his flat was slightly ajar.

He said, 'Give me the ignition key, Rodney.'

'Why?'

'Give.' When Rodney had handed over the key ring, David added, 'Just stay here while I check something. Do you no good to make a bolt for it. You couldn't carry all that wine at one go.'

He walked fast across the pavement and into the narrow hall. The door leading back to the office was shut. The door at the foot of his stairs had been splintered and forced open. Warily he went up the stairs, a tread at a time, making no sound. On the landing the door into the flat was open. He pushed it further open, very gently, and took one step through, poised on his toes, his arms hanging loose.

Without warning the side door into the lavatory was flung open. A very large man shouldered his way out and forced David into the sitting room. Another man who might have been his twin was there, ready to lend a hand and propel David right across the room into the far wall.

'You made a mistake, sonny. You don't write no letters, okay?'

'Go away,' said David.

'We got your word that no letters get written?'

David was reluctant to use his skills. They were too precious, too delicate, to be employed on bruisers of this nature, who would not understand any of the more refined techniques.

'Go away,' he said again, 'or I shall have to hurt you.'

'*You?* Who you think you're goin' to hurt?'

The first thug evidently felt he had displayed enough sweet reason and was now prepared to enjoy himself. He made a mighty swing at David. David moved his head fractionally, and his arm more freely. The man reeled backwards, cursing. Then the two of them piled in. A vase on the mantelpiece crashed to the floor. This enraged David: it was the only even halfway decent possession he had. He got a head jab into the neck of one of his attackers, feeling the man sag and reel away, stunned. Without pause he arm-locked the other, hauled him to the top of the stairs, and pitched him down the flight.

'Godalmighty,' said a familiar voice from the foot of the stairs. King, coming cautiously through from the office, tried to step back to avoid any further falling debris. The second thug, hauling himself up to his feet, took a swipe. King staggered backwards. Before he could be pursued into the office, David sprang down the stairs in three leaps and rushed the bruiser out into the street.

It took two more neatly placed blows to finish the man off. Rodney, watching from the Transit, made a move as if to get out, but then thought better of it.

King emerged again, rolling the groaning hulk of Frightener Mark I out to join his companion in the open air. Dusting his hands, he said, 'Nice work. I still think you're a lovely mover.'

David wiped a bloodstain away from the end of his nose.

'But that one serves you right,' said King. 'No more than you deserve.'

'What do you mean by that?'

'I'll tell you what I mean. Came by here half an hour ago to check up how you were making out, and what do I get? A telephone call from Mr Jansen Mowbray, that's what. Mr Devas is displeased. Approves of us one minute, disapproves the next. And why?'

'Don't tell me.'

'I bloody well will tell you. Mr Devas doesn't approve of folk who betray a client's confidential trust. Writing to the Foreign Office! What's wrong with your brain? What are you, a bloody anarchist?'

'It's immoral.'

'Dead right it's immoral, antagonizing a wealthy client. But since the trip has been called off, and since we seem to be in line for some payment on those wines, if we can . . . just a minute.' King stared up at the face behind the windscreen of the Transit. 'What's in there?'

'Rodney,' said David. 'Or Roger. Take your pick.'

'I can see that. What's in the *back*?'

'Wine. Lots of it.'

'Wine,' breathed King. 'Now you're talking.'

Before he could make a move, David took charge. He walked over to the van and said commandingly, 'Right, Rodney. If you'll step this way, we'll sort out all these invoices.'

King nodded approval. 'Even your tone of voice is getting a sort of aikido punch to it.'

'I think it's time I called you Ronald.'

'See what I mean? Not that I've ever stopped you.'

'Okay, Ronald. Clear your desk, and let's finish with our chum here.'

'And when we've finished,' said Ronald King sweetly, 'you will do me a special favour, David?'

'It depends.'

'You will go along to Lennie Teitelbaum and collect your new suit.'

'I don't know that it's ready yet.'

'*I* do,' said King. 'So go get it.'

The table was laid. Two pans stood on the cooker, and there was a bottle of wine close to the gas rings, warming up to a temperature which would be about right by the time Deirdre arrived. It was doubtful whether this was the right way to treat a great claret, but David was not too much concerned about any breach of the aesthetic rules: it was frankly not a great claret, just something of which the Bulgarians had no reason to be too ashamed.

He left the door ajar – not difficult, since the recent visitors had ensured that it would need some repairs before anyone could close it properly – and went into the bedroom.

There it was, on its hanger, covering the mirror in his second-hand wardrobe. A suit. Stripes, lapels, trouser creases and all. David reached out and touched it. The contact gave him no pleasure. It lacked the friendly lived-in and slept-in texture of the clothes to which he had been accustomed these recent years.

But this had to be his new image. He tried to think himself into it.

And into what Deirdre would say when she saw him. If there was nothing else, at least there would be her approval. He, Mr David Castle, was going to look respectable. She would not have to flinch at the prospect of introducing him to a barrister, or a judge, or some toffee-nosed friend. Or to her partner.

Not that David wanted to make an impression on that dreary partner of hers.

But Deirdre . . . just how much impression did he want to make there? He dodged round the question, but it kept coming back. Wanting his son in his own custody, still saying that he was prepared to marry Anne if she would be prepared to have him . . . and yet . . . Deirdre . . .?

Once again he shoved the thoughts to one side and forced himself to put the suit on.

The trouble with putting it on was that he had to take it off its hanger and away from the wardrobe mirror; and when he had put it on, he could see himself in it and in the mirror, and it was not what he had ever envisaged.

But later he could take it off. After they had eaten, and drunk the wine, and talked, he would take the damn thing off. And Deirdre, sweet-smelling, breathless, sweetly moving Deirdre, would take off her dress and . . .

He was going to have to sit down one evening, not with Deirdre but simply with himself, and ask himself what the hell this was all leading to – and try to find an honest answer.

There were footsteps on the landing, and the door opened, and she must have seen the condition of the door, for her voice was at once apprehensive: 'David? Are you in?'

Before she could panic and dash off to dial 999, he walked as confidently as he could manage out of the bedroom.

'Well? What do you think?' He tried to look nonchalant. He might even had tried to imitate Rodney Finch-Courteney if he had not regarded Rodney as such a drip. The best thing was simply to stand still, be himself, and wait for Deirdre's gasp of admiration.

She stared. He put his right hand in his pocket, then took it out again. The bottom of his left trouser leg seemed to have become snarled up in his shoe. He shuffled his feet and transferred his weight from one to the other.

And Deirdre started to laugh. She had a beautiful, rich, bubbling laugh.

But it was no time for laughter.

And there was no reason for it to go on so long, so helplessly.

It all went to prove what he had intuitively known all along. Dressed in his old jeans and that lovely frayed green jacket, and the shirt which had been a part of him since . . . well, since he had first got it snarled up in the hairs on his chest . . . he had appealed to Deirdre. That was his real self, and she had fallen for him. Or that was the way the evidence pointed, anyway. And without the gear, stark-naked, she had appreciated him. But put him in just the kind of suit she had pleaded with him to buy, just the sort of suit Ronald King had insisted on buying for him, and what happened?

She burst out laughing and went on laughing, that was what happened. She doubled up, and hiccuped, and said, 'Oh, no,' at least four times over.

Which just went to show.

II

Dale Danbury and Roger Gray had not proved hard to find. They were not long-term villains, not capable of running away, and not liable to put up a last savage fight. Any histrionic gestures that might be made were merely left-overs from the days when Dale Danbury had played the lead as Doctor Linden in the long-running TV soap opera *Orchard Lea*, supposedly an everyday tale of everyday life in a country parish.

Not that either Danbury or his companion of so many years looked like the residents of a country parish. Both in their mid-fifties, they had an air of limp aestheticism, outdated and somehow exuding an odour of mental mothballs. In their dark suits, high-collar shirts and broad, floppy ties they had for years practised a mannered disdain which was now fading into defeat and melancholy. No, they would certainly not present the Manor Agency with any major problems.

After an appraisal of the ground floor, Danbury led King and Castle up the stairs of the little two-up, two-down house, as genteel but as down at heel as its occupants. Roger Gray despondently brought up the rear.

In the principal bedroom Danbury waved a languid hand towards a kidney-shaped dressing table and stool. 'Hire purchase.' His sweeping, weary gesture took in a wardrobe, exercise rowing-machine, and a gas fire with what would have been a flickering coal-and-flame effect if it had been turned on. 'Hire purchase . . . hire purchase. The two oil paintings belong to a friend. The bed' – his hand came to rest affectionately on one of the brass knobs – 'we own.'

'Bed must be worth a few hundred,' observed King.

He detected a whimper in Gray's throat. 'I suppose if our

next destination is a debtor's prison, they'd supply bunks, wouldn't they?'

The small room next to the bedroom had been turned into an office, with a desk, bookshelves, and a typewriter.

'The typewriter is lease hired,' said Danbury at once. 'Has to go back anyway. Very little here of any use.'

'Nice lot of books.'

'Of no great value.'

King noted a large gilded statuette of Hercules carrying the world on his shoulders. It was a Globe Award for TV Personality of the Year, inscribed to Dale Danbury in honour of his role as Doctor Linden.

He said, 'That wouldn't be real gold?'

'No, it would not. And if it were, you still would not have it. I would go to my death rather than part with it.'

King took a last quick look around. 'Shall we return downstairs, gentlemen?'

'It's only our house,' said Gray peevishly. 'We do what *you* want.'

'I thought you said you rented it.'

'Fortunately that is the case,' said Danbury, 'or people like you would have had us out in the street years ago.'

King did not trouble to answer. He felt sorry for this poor, aimless pair; but it was not his job to feel too sorry for anyone. The sole object of his tour of the house had been to satisfy his own eyes that there were no major assets on the premises. Undoubtedly there was little of any value: certainly not enough to pay off their debts. They owed his client, London and South Recovery Services, seven thousand three hundred and eleven pounds; and London and South were in their turn acting for a money-lender. Every day that passed, the debt accumulated more interest, at the rate of twenty-eight per cent per annum. The prospects were not good – for Danbury and Gray, or for King and Castle.

David Castle said sympathetically, 'Let's be practical. There's nothing in this house which will fetch any great price, and your work prospects as an actor are currently poor. But maybe there's something else. Are you in the will of an ageing relative, perhaps?'

Trust him to hark back to his old pursuits, thought King sceptically.

'What an absurd idea,' said Danbury loftily.

'Are you sure there aren't some other objects, not necessarily here in the house, that might have some value you've overlooked?'

'We have extended the courtesy of showing you the house. That, I'm afraid, is the end of it.'

'I'm sorry.' King was sharp and far from sorry. 'It is not. It's the beginning of it. You owe a lot of money and I wish to collect it.'

'What do you want us to do?' demanded Gray. 'Go out on the street and try some armed robbery?'

Danbury suddenly did a double take, with a turn of the head known, some years back, to every devoted viewer in the country. Then the head went gallantly back. His eyes became dewy with the urge to self-sacrifice.

'We do have an asset,' he announced.

Gray stared. 'Dale, you couldn't let yourself—'

'The last.' Danbury was not to be deflected from his performance.

'Let's be hearing it,' said King.

'I believe that with it we could possibly pay your people off and still have perhaps a couple of thousand left over for ourselves.'

'I'm still listening.'

'I take it you did view me in the role of Doctor Linden in *Orchard Lea?*'

'I did catch one or two of the shows.'

Gray bridled. 'I don't think we like it being called "shows". It was a twice-weekly television *drama.*'

'Oh, is that what it was?'

'After I had recorded the first thirty episodes' – Dale Danbury was staring back into a radiant past – 'I splashed out. Believing the series would run a dozen years instead of just three, I purchased an American Ford Mustang car which I arranged to be repainted in metallic pink.'

David looked interested. 'Pink?'

Gray smiled and nodded. 'If you caught only one or two of the "shows", as you put it, Mr King, you may be unclear about the importance of this pink Mustang.'

'For a period of years,' Danbury took up the tale again, 'my Mustang was unquestionably the most famous and most photographed automobile in the country.'

'So?'

'There's now an industry in memorabilia,' said Gray. 'Don't tell me that among the fifteen million who regularly watched Dale there isn't one rich enough to pay *anything* for that car.'

'You've still got it?' David was growing more and more enthusiastic. 'May we see it?'

'It's down the road in a lockup.' Gray turned towards the door. 'I'll be glad to show you.'

'No,' said Dale Danbury petulantly: '*I'll* show them.'

Before Gray could object, he bustled King and Castle out of the front door and slammed it to with one hand, hurrying down the street. The neighbouring houses were very much the same as the one they had just left: a row of little cottages left over from an age before the Victorian additions to Battersea, and now huddled below higher terraces as if fearful of being noticed. Some had tiny gardens, in one of which a stooped old woman of about seventy was fiddling with some flowers in pots. She looked slyly up as the three men passed.

'Good morning, Mrs Chalmers,' said Danbury without any noticeable warmth.

'How's your *friend* today?' she said, and sniggered.

After they had gone on a few paces, Danbury said, 'Why are people so unpleasant nowadays? You used to be able to associate old people with olde-worlde charm.'

They reached a yard set back from the street, lined with what had once been an attempt at a row of lockup garages. The area must have declined, for few of them had any doors left and most of them were empty. In the shadows of one, with a few glints of light through holes in the roof, was a very battered metallic pink Mustang. King observed that the registration number was DAN 100. That was one point in its favour, anyway.

David, disappointed, said, 'It's a total wreck.'

'Mostly rust,' King agreed.

'Sotheby's auctions?' Danbury was warming to the possibilities, his faith rekindled. Already he was writing a whole new scenario for himself. 'What about the Beatles' memorabilia?'

'I don't remember any rusty guitars,' said David.

'Let us concede that it needs a few hundred for a good respray. But it's got to be worth thousands.' Danbury took King's arm with long, slightly caressing fingers. 'Sit in it. Go on – sit in the Danbury pink Mustang. Something not many people have ever been allowed to do. Something to tell your kids about.'

'I don't have kids.'

'A few hundred for a respray and rechrome.' There was no stopping him now. 'She'll be like new. A gleaming classic. Totally irresistible. Now, we must make some contact. It'll involve an investment by you, of course.'

'What?'

'Who's going to pay for the respray? We're flat broke. You know that. But do you know that the cherished number, DAN 100, is possibly worth in itself two thousand pounds?'

King was dazed. The abandoned car was not an impressive sight. But in this crazy world there could well be something in what Danbury was claiming. Thoughtfully he began to stroll back towards the house. Danbury fell into step.

From a side road came the shriek and jangle of a ghetto blaster. A gang of youths, black and white, were dancing along the pavement and in the corners of house doorways, in the gutter and halfway across the street. The amplified uproar bruised King's ears. Then there was silence. One of them was bent over the blaster, changing the cassette. Into the silence came the wail of a police siren. It had the same effect as a starting pistol. The youths raced off – two of them down the street, one around the corner, two more over a fence and round a back alley, and one, swinging the blaster, madly off up the street in the opposite direction. The police car appeared, hesitated on the corner, then swung past Danbury and his two companions.

'Nice quiet residential neighbourhood,' commented King. Now it was his own turn to feel nostalgic: he felt the tingle of pursuit, the adrenalin rush as you raced after a quarry and finally cornered him. . . . Regretfully he wrenched his attention back to matters in hand.

When they reached the house, the front door was half open. Danbury clicked his tongue as he led the way in.

'Well?' said Roger Gray hopefully to King.

Danbury said, 'Why did you come out and leave the front door open?'

'I haven't been near the front door.'

'It was open when we came in just this minute.'

'Then you can't have shut it properly when you left.'

Danbury appeared to be on the verge of indulging in a tiff. Then, like King, he forced himself to concentrate on more important things.

'Show them the scrapbook,' he ordered.

Roger was only too happy to oblige. He dug into a large cupboard and produced a leatherbound scrapbook stuffed with pictures of the Mustang and Dale Danbury. He sat in it contemplating the beauties of nature in a country lane. He leaned nonchalantly on it beside the gateway to an orchard. He strode across the pavement towards it from the steps of a Park Lane hotel. At a Motor Show he leaned on the bonnet, part of a special exhibit along with two girls whose legs went on longer than was reasonable. Roger snatched that page over with a little sniff.

King said, 'I get the picture. Now, can I take a borrow of it?'

'Go away and make enquiries,' said Danbury, still in a confident mood. 'Find out how much to respray and so on, value of the number . . . then we'll talk again.'

He had taken charge of the proceedings. King was tempted to protest, but felt he would achieve more by going away and thinking the matter over in a calmer atmosphere.

As they got into the Rover he said, 'What d'you think?'

'Do I think there's seven thousand three hundred pounds plus a few extras in a rusting pink Mustang with a silly number plate owned by a two-dimensional face from last year but God knows how many? The answer is, the world's so crazy that it's probably yes.'

Ronald King thought so too. He also thought he knew someone who might offer corroboration.

The Military Memorabilia shop in Fulham had a window bristling with Japanese swords, American bayonets, German helmets, and a drapery of ribbons and medals. Inside, you needed to duck your head to avoid being impaled by sinister objects hanging from the ceiling.

Wallace Heal, the proprietor, had not seen Ronnie King for a few years. That might have accounted for his quite genuine, spontaneous beam of welcome and the hearty handshake.

'Well, look who it is. Come through . . . coffee? . . . with a drop of the hard?'

'We've just come from elevenses.' King gingerly fingered the blade of a Gurkha kukris. 'This stuff selling?'

'Very handy for seeing off the mother-in-law.'

Having dodged the vaguest likelihood of ever having such a creature in his neighbourhood, King shrugged that one aside and followed Heal into the rear room of the shop. David sidled in after them. Wallace Heal, who had the podgy but shrewd features of a Petticoat Lane stall-keeper, assessed him briefly and implied with one twitch of the nose that if King wanted to flog him this creature, he wouldn't have it even on the most favourable part-exchange terms.

It was time, thought King grimly, that David Castle came out into the daylight in one of those suits so carefully selected for him.

He said briskly, 'Right, Wal. It's memorabilia I want to discuss. It's a word that's everywhere now, yes?'

'It's an industry.'

'And it's true that a lot of silly prices are being paid for silly things?' David contributed.

Heal continued to look at his old mate, King. 'You got something in the memorabilia line?'

'Possibly.'

Heal moved some swords off a chair so that he could sit down. 'Ritual hara-kiri swords,' he explained, 'as used by the Japs when the VAT men came round.'

David once again looked interested. Determined not to be

deflected, King pushed on. 'Did you ever watch a television programme called *Orchard Lea?*'

'Off and on,' Heal admitted.

'The main part was a Doctor Linden—'

'Dale Danbury. Yes. Whatever happened to him?'

'He had a pink Mustang car.'

'Right.'

'Still has it,' said King. 'He wants to sell it.'

Wallace Heal began to show signs of interest. Unlike David's interest, it had the hint of money behind it. 'He does?'

'It's got a cherished number. DAN 100.'

'That's nice to hear. You offering some sort of deal? Want to name a price?'

'Just want to talk,' said King.

They talked.

The next port of call was at London and South Recovery Services in Pimlico, later that afternoon. You had to admit that 'Recovery Services' gave off a more fashionable ring than 'Debt Collection Agency'; and King derived a fine appreciative sensation from the glass-walled reception area, the deep chairs, and the no-expense-spared swirl of the receptionist's hairdo. This was it. He would have been prepared to bet that this lot were collecting debts in millions. This was what he was working towards, and he was in a hurry to get there.

Miss Wilmott couldn't have led them along a carpeted corridor the way this girl was doing. And that was not only because the Manor Debt Collection Agency was pretty thin on the ground when it came to carpets: Miss Wilmott was also comparatively pretty thin around the bottom.

Another large reception room, more glass walling and a luxuriance of deep leather armchairs, and the cooing voice said, 'Mr Renton will be with you in a moment.'

As soon as she had swayed off into the bright blue yonder, King said, 'One word to you. You be appropriately servile and businesslike with Mr Renton. If we pull off this Dale Danbury recovery, there's obviously more work here for us.'

David lowered himself into one of the chairs and found it pleasing. One or two aspects, however, were not to his liking.

'I don't understand why you've started a debt collecting agency,' he said, 'if all you want to do is work for another debt collecting company. I mean, working for a lesser commission than if you were working for yourself . . .'

'Co-operation,' said King. 'A bit beyond you, that, isn't it? Look round you, lad. These are the big boys. This is the glamour end of the market. We play it their way, some of it rubs off, we move up in the world.' He found a chair and acknowledged that its comfort took some beating. 'I reckon DAN 100 can have all the donks knocked out and a quick once-over for five hundred. Look at that four hundred thousand paid at auction, few months ago, for that Bugatti. Look at that press cutting book: I tell you, that Mustang was a star, a gorgeous pink star.'

'Somehow I knew,' said David, 'that at some point in my association with you we'd end up selling second-hand cars.'

Renton summoned them into his office.

He was a young-faced man with iron-grey hair which had been brushed back austerely to form one virtually seamless swathe like a narrow steel bonnet. His lips were thin, his eyes narrow and very pale as if bleached from too much staring aggressively into the sun.

His voice was clipped and precise. 'I have had a word with some associates. The pink car seems a possibility. We would like you to pursue it. Any negotiation between you and Mr Danbury must not, however, suggest in any way that acceptance of such a property in part payment will be agreed until a reasonable price is realized.'

'Quite so, Mr Renton.' Ronald King was learning to be deferential while implying great reserves of know-how.

'The number, DAN 100, should also be considered as a potentially valuable part of the deal. We are happy to let you continue down this avenue of enquiry.'

'Right, Mr Renton.'

'Then I think we understand each other. Before you go, though, could I have a word in private?'

King looked at David. David looked blandly back at him. King tried to jerk a discreet thumb. It took three separate, mountingly obvious jerks before David got the message and slouched out of the office.

Renton said, 'Now, Mr King, your company could be very useful to us on a long-term basis.'

'Very pleased to hear that, Mr Renton.'

'It would be a considerable asset to have an organization like yours handling some of the more straightforward cases while my main team concentrates on the international scene. We have quite a reputation there.' Renton closed his hands, the tips of his fingers pressing against each other, and looked suitably reverent. 'I would point out, however, that even in the purely domestic market, our clients tend to come in the A and B categories. I'm saying that among the people we chase for debts are lords and earls and suchlike.'

'Quite, sir.'

Renton gazed past him through the glass, where David Castle's lank shape looked like an abstract sculpture in the middle of the stylish reception area. 'That gentleman is in your permanent employ?'

'He is.'

'To be frank, Mr King, if that chap went off to some stately home on a brief originating from this office, they'd probably call the police. His appearance, Mr King—'

'You are not to worry on any account regarding my employee's appearance,' said King hastily. 'He wears the gear that goes with whatever job he's engaged on – so he doesn't look too conspicuous.'

'Conspicuous?' said Renton dubiously.

'I assure you, Mr Renton, I've had him fitted out by my personal tailor for the better-class investigations.'

'I'm relieved to hear it.' Renton stood up and held out his hand. 'I'll get our contracts manager to draw up a draft agreement for our working relationship, and then we'll talk again. In the meantime, you'll get that Dale Danbury matter sewn up?'

'It's in safe hands.'

King went out with a spring in his step. David followed him through the outer doors, which purred shut behind them, and down the steps.

'What were you two waffling on about in there?'

'He was very impressed by us,' said King. 'One thing, though – you've taken delivery of those suits, haven't you?'

'Yes.'

'I'd suggest you start wearing one when you emerge each day from your burrow. And now I'm going to drop you at a hairdresser's.'

'What? I only go to the barber's once a quarter.'

'You don't surprise me. But I'm not talking about a barber. I'm talking about a skilled hairdresser with bags of ideas. And' – he glanced at David's locks, too tangled even to twitch in the breeze – 'with bags of courage.'

King began humming to himself as they drove away. It really did look as if things were beginning to go his way. He felt good. Manor Debt was making real progress, moving onwards and upwards. Tomorrow he might even go out and buy himself a bowler hat.

By the following morning he had forgotten the bowler hat, but remembered the need to fix the paint job for the Mustang. With that settled, he headed for the office to dictate a letter of agreement which Dale Danbury would have to sign. The prospect of this was enough to dampen his good spirits. Dictating to Miss Wilmott was not one of the great joys of the day.

She looked pointedly at her watch when he came in.

'Calls?' he said tersely, to put her in her place.

'Er, yes. Four. I think.'

'You *think*?'

'A Mr Hatchard, and Mr Peter Heron. Or it may have been Herring. And a Mr Forsyth who asked for an appointment, Thursday if possible. Oh, and there was—'

'You've written all this down?' King was impatient to get past her and into the chair behind his desk.

'I can remember most of the details.'

'When you get a telephone call,' King erupted, 'ask for the name and number and the nature of the enquiry. And write them down. And put the piece of paper on my desk.'

'While you've been going on like this,' said Miss Wilmott defensively, 'I've saved the most—'

'I am *not* "going on like this"!'

'The most important message,' she said. 'It was from Dale Danbury. He didn't have to give his name. I'd recognize that voice anywhere. I don't think I missed one minute of *Orchard Lea* in all the—'

'Just tell me what he said.'

'He sounded terrible. He said he must see you "utterly urgent". Those were his own words: "utterly urgent".'

12

Dale Danbury had been crying. His eyes were red and his hands shook uncontrollably as he scattered crumbs over the tiny lawn. He hardly bothered to look at the birds coming down greedily from the square dovecote set against the end wall.

'Right,' said King. 'What's the panic?'

'They've taken Roger.' There were tears in his voice. 'They just march in here, carry him off, throw him into their car – positively *throw* him, it was *brutal* – and . . . and . . .'

'Take it easy, Mr Danbury,' said David Castle gently. 'Tell us exactly how it happened, right from the beginning.'

Danbury gulped. 'One, you and your pal arrive and we go to look at my Mustang. Two, we return and Roger is here, all quite normal. Three, you leave. Four, minutes later the police barge in and arrest him. *Arrest* him . . . carry poor Roger off!'

'Arrest him for what?'

'I went round to ask whatever they thought they were up to, and they said that while the three of us were out looking at the car, he went off and stole a stereo. Went off with some coloured boys . . . Harding's Hi-Fi on Lavender Hill . . . *coloured* boys, if I've told him once I . . .'

Danbury was growing incoherent again. David spent a moment or two calming him down, and gradually the facts emerged – or what passed for facts.

The basic story was a familiar enough situation in that area, in this day and age. A gang of six had been seen weaving in a crocodile down Lavender Hill, past the shops. Four of them stopped outside Harding's Hi-Fi and pressed their noses to the window; the other two, one black and one white, went inside. They asked for a ghetto blaster priced at ninety-nine pounds ninety-five pence to be removed from the window for closer inspection – and suddenly tossed it from one to the other, made a dash for the door, and got away while their four mates pulled the door shut and held it for just long enough to mess up any possible pursuit.

'They must have been that lot swanning around the road when we were on our way back,' said King. 'But where does Gray fit into this?'

'They say he was with them.'

'At Lavender Hill?' David looked hopelessly at a dove approaching a crumb near his big toe. 'But that's five minutes there and five minutes back. We weren't away from the house much more than five minutes all told.'

'They say they have a positive identification.'

'They can't have.'

'And,' Danbury said wretchedly, 'in our front salon, they went straight in and found a big grey hi-fi thing with its price tag still on.'

David shook his head. There was no way Roger Gray could have belted down to Lavender Hill, lifted a stereo blaster, and got back here while the three of them were just round the corner. If he had done any nicking, it must have been before King and Castle ever got to the house.

'The fact is' – Danbury was piling the agony on himself – 'Roger has been seeing young boys. I've been furious with him. I mean . . . well, you know, nowadays, the *things* that he could pick up.'

Including a hundred quid's worth of hi-fi, thought David; then did his best to unthink it.

King said, 'Listen, you're not to worry. We know that has to be nonsense. We have a fine lawyer, a Miss Deirdre Aitken. We'll get her moving.'

David started. This was the first he had heard of Deirdre being promoted to the status of the Manor Debt Collection Agency's lawyer.

'David, you go into the house and ring Deirdre. I'll get to the local station and talk to the CID. Meet me down there. And while you're waiting, you have the log book out on the car and a short note from Mr Danbury here giving me permission to sell it and recover the debt owed to our client. I meant to have it typed up in the office, but with this flap—'

'While you keep *talking*,' wailed Danbury, 'Roger is in a *cell*.'

'You do that little thing for me, I'll get Roger out and back here.' King went back through the house, and was gone.

David was pumping up the rear tyre of his recently regenerated moped when Deirdre's red mini slid to a halt behind him, across the road from the police station. He straightened up to greet her.

She said, 'When did I become your company's legal eagle? I think I should have been told.'

'Don't you want to make money out of us?'

'You, I don't mind. It's King. I don't specialize in criminal law, and he's a criminal.'

'I wouldn't say that.'

'I would.' She indicated the moped. 'And when are you going to get rid of this thing?'

'This machine functions perfectly well,' said David with dignity. 'It does what it was designed to do. It works.'

'It could kill. Perhaps you or some pedestrian.' Deirdre gave up. 'So what's happening here?'

'King's inside, trying to speak to somebody.'

'The name of the arrested?'

'Gray. With an "a".'

Deirdre switched tracks again. 'Have you talked to Hodinett any further?'

'I was going to,' he hedged. 'Later. It's been a bit hectic.'

'David, your court case is now just three weeks away. It should be more important to you than hounding debtors.'

'Of course it is.'

'Some character witnesses are a key factor in your situation. We're trying to sell you as a first-class person with first-class contacts. Go find a phone box, and arrange for the two of us to see Hodinett today.'

'When I get back to the office—'

'Do it now.'

He watched her cross the road and go up the steps into the

police station. For a moment he thought of following, finding out what was going on and what progress King was making. There were times when King needed not so much moral support as a moral watchdog. But then he thought of Deirdre's warm eyes which could turn so cold and accusing; and he went off to phone Mr Hodinett.

Mr Hodinett was out. He would be back, but then he would be going out again. Was there anywhere Mr Castle could be reached?

David gave the office number, and hurried back there.

He had been at his desk about ten minutes when the phone rang. He picked it up, expecting to hear Hodinett's bumbling tones. Instead there was King snapping into his ear. 'What are you doing back at the office?'

'I'm waiting for a call.'

'From Danbury?'

'From Hodinett.'

'For God's sake, stick to one job at a time. We've got a hostile witness. If I heard it right, the name is Mrs Chalmers, near neighbour of Danbury.'

'The one he spoke to when we went off to see the Mustang.'

'So it was. Good. It shouldn't be too much of an intellectual challenge for you to remember the house.'

'Where does she come into it?'

'Says she saw Roger run into the house with the nicked stereo. Lying old cow. It just isn't possible.'

For once King and Castle were in perfect accord. David knew it wasn't possible, it didn't fit; and he was ready and willing to put a few questions to that sour-faced old creature they had passed only yesterday.

Mrs Chalmers was not pottering about with her plants today. Along the side of the house he saw the edge of a sheet billowing in the wind. He went along the path and found the old woman with three clothes pegs between her teeth.

She glared at him, obviously wondering whether to scream for help. In the time it took her to extricate the pegs as a preparatory move, David said, 'I'm David Castle. I'd like to have a word with you about a neighbour of yours. A Mr Gray – the police have arrested him.'

Mrs Chalmers turned away, but found herself entangled in a heavy wet blanket. David moved round to help her. As she puffed her way out and dabbed at her cheeks, she said, 'What's it got to do with me?'

'Well, it's a bit puzzling really. I mean, I don't think he could have done it – stolen that stereo, which is what he's accused of. I wasn't with him, but I was with his friend Mr Danbury.'

Mrs Chalmers pursed her lips. She had black little button eyes, malicious and bright with disapproval. 'So?'

'Well, it's very confusing.' David was taking it quietly and carefully. 'Because we were only away from Mr Gray five minutes, and the police say that in five minutes he was able to get to Lavender Hill, steal this thing, and return. That is, if *your* evidence is reliable.'

'You've got a nerve, young man. Why shouldn't I be reliable?'

'I don't think he could have done all that in five minutes.'

'Nobody's asking what you think. I know what I saw.'

'You're sure of that?'

'Why shouldn't I be? Running up the road, into the house – door open, all ready and planned, if you ask me.'

'Oh, dear.' David looked up reflectively at the array of table napkins and handkerchiefs fluttering on the line. 'I'm a little upset for Mr Gray. And a little worried for you.'

'What d'you mean, worried for me?'

'Well, Mrs Chalmers, if you made a mistake – I'm not saying you did, mind you – but if somehow you have . . . then Mr Gray isn't the robber, and the real robber must be out there. On the loose,' he added in a sepulchral tone.

'On the loose?'

'As you were looking at the real robber and thinking he was Mr Gray, he probably spotted *you*. That means he could come back here.'

Mrs Chalmers put out a hand to steady herself, and almost brought the clothes-line pole down. 'Why should he?'

'Well, he'll want to talk to you. Sound you out. That's logical. He'll want to convince you not to change your mind – your story about how you definitely, *very definitely* saw Mr Gray steal the stereo.'

'I didn't see that. Didn't see him actually steal it, or . . . and I didn't say *very* definitely about anything . . .'

'Mrs Chalmers,' said David unctuously. 'I'm not the police. But I can stop this thief from turning up and bothering you. Only I need to know who he is.'

Mrs Chalmers clicked her tongue against her teeth; wiped her hands on her apron and then wiped them again; and looked at the few pieces of washing left in the basket at her feet. Nothing seemed to offer her any inspiration. At last she said, 'I didn't want to make trouble. I mean, I've got no time for men like that, but I wouldn't . . . that is, you see, my memory's not so good as it was. I mean, you don't know where you are sometimes.'

'It must make things difficult. Sometimes.'

'Now, when I come to think about it, maybe it wasn't the poofter. Yes, now I've remembered something.'

'You have?'

'There was a black bloke. He was sort of running past, just about that very time. I don't know that he was carrying that stereo thing, but he *could* have been.'

She was imploring him to forgive her and believe her. Before she started getting eager enough to invent further details and blur the issue, David said:

'And you might know who it was?'

'If it's who I'm thinking . . . yes, it's that fellow with the hole-in-the-wall garage. Morley's Garage.'

Mrs Chalmers hesitated, but had gone too far now to turn back. 'Malcolm,' she said. 'Don't know the rest, but they're always shouting and yelling "Malcolm" after him, and . . . oh, you get no peace round here nowadays. I don't know what the world's coming to.'

David favoured her with one brief sympathetic smile, and went off in search of Morley's Garage, which proved to be little more than two petrol pumps and a repair bay within the arch of a viaduct.

Someone was working underneath a car. One long leg sprawled out, showing enough ankle to confirm that the skin was black.

David prodded the ankle. There was a curse, and the man came writhing out. 'What you want?'

'Are you Malcolm?'

'Yes.' He pushed himself upright with one hand against the wing of the car. He was tall, and his arms looked very strong.

'Well, someone I know has been arrested by the police,' said David mildly. 'They say he stole a stereo, but I'm sure you're the one who stole it.'

There was a long, menacing pause. Malcolm still had one hand on the car, but his knuckles were whitening and his head was thrusting forward. 'And who the hell are you?'

'The name is Castle. David Castle. And I'm accusing you of the theft of stereo equipment from—'

'Go away. And quick.' Without another word Malcolm pushed past him and strode across to a wooden hut which served as an office. The door slammed behind him.

David took a deep breath, walked to the hut, and let himself in.

Malcolm turned. 'You didn't hear me, man?'

'I heard you.'

'Then you get out of here.'

'We have to talk about Mr Gray and the stolen stereo,' said David patiently. 'The one you stole.'

Malcolm shouldered past him again, this time on his way out. He was a fast mover, was Malcolm, but an aimless one. 'Last chance,' he snapped over his shoulder. 'Leave this place.'

'We have to talk about the stereo.'

Malcolm stooped and snatched up a section of exhaust pipe. He lobbed it towards David, whose automatic reaction was to put his hands out and catch it. As he did so, Malcolm grabbed the next nearest thing that came to hand – a long metal wrench. He swung it against the side of David's head.

David gave up arguing, and went down into darkness.

Deirdre ought to have been used to seeing David with gashes, purple bruises and similar adornments, but she could not repress an instinctive wince when he showed up with a bandage round his head and an angry red inflammation down his cheek.

Before she could make some tart remark, he put the ball in her court by demanding, 'Well, have you got Mr Gray released?'

'Not yet.'

'But he's innocent. We know he is. If they've charged him with—'

'That's the point. They haven't charged him, so no bail. They say they *will* charge him, and they'll put an identity parade together. Meanwhile he's requested some other lawyer, some pal somewhere in Buckinghamshire, and they say they can't locate him.'

'You know, in the last six months one has formed the definite impression that the law is a professional, unrelenting, twenty-four-hours-a-day ass.'

'Thanks, I'm sure.'

'The man's innocent, and you can't get him released. Fat chance *I'm* going to stand in court, if this is the way the law works, upside down and back to front.'

'Speaking of which, where do we meet Mr Hodinett?'

The venue confirmed over the phone was a bowling green some half-mile from the office which David remembered so well. He had never known, during his employment there, that his employer had been a bowls fanatic. That must have been the explanation for his frequent absences: David had assumed that Hodinett was doggedly pursuing inheritors, just as he was, but now he realized that the old man's afternoons were passed in the company of geriatric friends.

They stood at the side of the green and watched Hodinett, puffing, stoop and despatch a bowl. He puffed along in its wake; but the bowl went short. Hodinett waved surrender to two men at the far end of the green, and then found himself face to face with David Castle.

'Well played, sir,' said David.

'Indeed? Very hard to see how I could have lost more ignominiously, Whittaker.'

'Castle, sir. David Castle. I don't think you've met Deirdre Aitken, my lawyer.'

There was an unexpected gleam in Hodinett's rheumy eye. He looked Deirdre shamelessly up and down, and chuckled his appreciation. 'Lawyer, eh? Thought you must be his nurse. Your client seems to have a habit of walking into lamp posts.' He took Deirdre's arm and began walking her towards the clubhouse. Hardly deigning even to glance at David, he said, 'What d'you need a lawyer for, eh? Are you suing me?'

'Mr Hodinett, we spoke. A couple of weeks ago. And on the phone this morning.'

'Refresh my memory, young man.'

'I rang your office, and you rang back, and that's why we're here. You invited us.'

Hodinett smiled at Deirdre and squeezed her closer to him as they went into the clubhouse. When they reached the bar he insisted that she have a sherry. David waited to be asked what he would like. He was not asked. But Hodinett did include him in the gracious wave which indicated that they should be seated at a table in the window.

Deirdre said, slowly and distinctly, 'David is going to court in about three weeks from now. He wants to gain some kind of custody order concerning his child, who is about to be put up for adoption.'

'His illegitimate child,' Hodinett recalled with an effort. Reluctantly he switched his gaze from Deirdre to David. 'Whittaker had a similar problem with a divorce from his Turkish wife. You remember Whittaker?'

'No, sir.'

'Never could keep anything in your head for five minutes, could you? Now what was I saying? Oh, yes. Whittaker. There was a fight over custody of both children and a Siamese cat. Poor boy, he got only the moggie.'

David could almost hear Deirdre groaning inwardly. She kept her voice steady. 'Mr Hodinett, it's very simple. Since David left the Royal Navy—'

'Didn't know you were a matelot,' said Hodinett, interested. 'RAF chappie myself. Service mainly in the African campaign.'

'Africa, sir? Really?'

'Rommel and all that. I came very near to seeing off the legendary Herr General. I was on patrol, Spitfire, over Wadi Halfa—'

'Since David left the navy,' said Deirdre heavily, 'his history of employment has been very sketchy. Opportunities these last few years have generally been poor.'

'But he left my employment, Miss Aitken.' About this, at any rate, Hodinett was clear. 'As Mr Denton, God rest his soul, said on one occasion of our friend Whittaker here, "Gone tomorrow almost before here today."'

'Castle, sir,' said David, 'and I was with you nearly a whole year.'

'Ah, only that? I thought it was longer.'

Deirdre put her glass down on the table with some force. 'Mr Hodinett, please. Are you prepared, in the first place, to sign some form of letter which would be a character reference for David, which could be produced during his coming court appearance? And in the second place, would you be magnanimous enough to appear in court, if so requested, to give David a verbal character reference?'

'Magnanimous?' Hodinett tried the word over and rather liked the sound of it. Then he said, 'Who is this David?'

'Me.'

Hodinett stared. 'You? I'm to appear in court to give *you* a character reference?'

Deirdre opened her case and took out a sheet of paper. 'I've drafted the note which I think we could use as a discussion basis. Or perhaps you'd be prepared to sign now?' She pushed it across the table. David craned his neck to read the contents at the same time as Hodinett.

> To Whom it may Concern.
> I was the employer of David Castle for a year, and during this time the standard of his work and general attitude was excellent and highly conscientious.
> Signed . . . .

Hodinett mouthed the words silently to himself, with mounting incredulity. David and Deirdre held their breath. After what seemed an eternity Hodinett said, 'Did you know that I was a closet Scottish Nationalist, young lady?'

'No.'

'Which means I have an historic contempt for English law, English courts, and the entire Sassenach legal process. Which also means that I am perfectly happy to perjure myself by signing this appalling document.' He took out a pen and signed with a flourish. 'As to appearing in court, we shall have to discuss that nearer the time. I'm a very busy man.' He glared at David, daring him to dispute this. 'Also our bowling team has some major fixtures coming up. People who have never played bowls cannot understand why Sir Walter Raleigh took time to finish his game before turning his attention to the Armada.'

'Drake,' said David without thinking.

'What was that, laddie?'

'Nothing, sir.'

'Those who play,' concluded Hodinett, 'realize Sir Walter had his priorities exactly right. If the court case coincides with a fixture, then as far as I'm concerned Whittaker can be sent down for twelve years for this kidnapping, or whatever it is he's done.'

'Not a kidnapping, sir,' David protested. 'A custody order. And . . .'

Deirdre was on her feet, clutching his arm and forcing him up beside her. With her free hand she picked up the sheet of paper.

'Thank you very much indeed, Mr Hodinett, for signing this. Greatly appreciated. We'll be in touch.'

Hodinett wistfully studied her legs as she led David towards the door.

13

It was not so much a matter of killing two birds with one stone as of luring one bird down with bait for another. Ronald King thought of the doves in Dale Danbury's garden, and thought of Dale Danbury's debts and Dale Danbury's desires; and saw how the whole thing could be neatly and profitably settled.

On the recommendation of his friend Heal he made his way to the forecourt of Howard's Specialist Automobiles, which lived gratifyingly up to its name: King wandered with a wistful expression down a line of Bentleys and Mercs, 635 BMWs and Morgans, culminating in a gleaming silver Rolls. The number-plates were in keeping: distinctive, personal, expensive.

As he leaned into the interior of the Rolls and drooled over the sheer intoxicating smell of it, a voice at his shoulder said, 'Looking for anything special, sir?'

'If I were, I've come to the right place.' King straightened up. 'Ronald King.'

'Ah, Wallace's old mate. Told me you'd be along. How's his Nazi flags selling?'

'Like hot swastikas.' King looked along the line of bonnets. 'So all your cars have cherished numbers.'

'Take this car you've just been looking at.' Howard tapped the radiator. 'It's a nice Roller. Seventy-four thousand miles, full service history, worth twelve thousand seven-fifty at best. But I stick a cherished number like this DEL 661 on it . . .' Howard grinned up into the benevolent heavens. 'Well, the number cost me six hundred, and some punter called Del, or initials D.E.L., is going to see or be told about my three inserts in *Exchange and Mart*, and he'll be in here clutching fifteen grand to hand over.'

'That a fact?'

'It is. And what's the cherished number,' asked Howard, 'that's come *your* way?'

'DAN 100.'

'Could be interesting. Mm, I'd say those were sought-after initials.'

'How much d'you think it's worth?'

'You mean what would I pay you for it?' Howard smoothly corrected him.

'That's what I mean, yes.'

'You got a log book?'

'I'm getting it.'

'I'd give you two thousand one hundred.'

King felt a tingle of pleasure. He had to congratulate himself on the way he was handling this little business.

'I'll get the log book,' he promised, 'and you've got a sale.'

Next stop was at Dale Danbury's. He had expected the stricken man to be still pacing up and down the garden, scattering crumbs and moistening a few of them with his tears. Instead he found only a cleaning lady, banging about the place and grunting to herself. She had not expected visitors. She wasn't paid to cope with visitors. Yes, Mr Danbury was out. And where Mr Danbury went when he went out was Mr Danbury's business. Could be anywhere.

It took King about a minute and a half to apply tactics of coaxing and bullying which elicited the information that sometimes Mr Danbury went swimming at the pool the other side of the common.

King found the pool. At this time of day it was not crowded. A few office workers were snatching a brief break, and two children were rousing echoes at the shallow end. Danbury's silvery locks bobbing above the surface and making slow progress towards the side were easily identifiable.

He showed no pleasure at identifying King. 'What are you doing here? I do expect my privacy to be respected. I need my privacy.' But then, brushing a hand through his damp hair, he said, 'What's the news?'

'Good news.'

'Tell me.'

'I think the combination of the refurbished motor and the cherished number looks like paying off your total debts to our client.'

'I'm not talking about that,' raged Danbury shrilly. 'I'm talking about Roger. Is he charged? Is he coming out of that police cell? You recommended a lawyer – what's she doing?'

'I'm sure that right at this moment she's hard at it.'

'I can't believe that man, who is totally innocent, is still incarcerated and nobody's getting anything useful done about it.'

'They say he'll be charged,' was all King had to offer.

'When?'

'There *is* the problem of the stereo found in your front room – and the witness.'

'Witness . . . stereo . . . lies, utter lies! What are you going to do?'

Danbury had hauled himself out and was groping for a bathrobe. King let him grope. After a long pause he said, 'I need the log book. And obviously a note from you. And of course a set of ignition keys.'

Danbury's fury was bubbling over. 'I've forgotten your name,' he said venomously, 'but whatever it is, you'll get nothing. You have been unable to get Roger released. You serve no useful purpose whatsoever. I am not now prepared even to consider giving you my automobile. Or anything else. Simply go away!'

King was tempted to lift the man bodily and chuck him back into the pool. But that would have solved nothing, and nor would less physical measures. Danbury was in far too emotional a state to be dealt with rationally.

He left. There had been a hitch in his nice, smooth calculations. Unable to take his frustration out on Danbury, who somehow still had to be made to come up with the goods, he headed back towards the office to let off steam at Miss Wilmott and David Castle.

Miss Wilmott had to bear the brunt of it. David was out, and had left no details of his whereabouts. So what the hell was he doing, and where was he doing it?

King dragged open the drawer in his filing cabinet, looked at the whisky bottle, and opted for the indigestion tablets.

David returned doggedly to the garage under the viaduct. It looked as unappetizing as when he had first seen it, and Malcolm was unlikely to be any friendlier. But David was going to go back in there, and this time there would be an end to the nonsense.

A pity people couldn't be sweet and reasonable . . .

Only then, of course, he would be out of a job.

There were five West Indians rattling and banging away in the workshop: or, at least, four of them were hard at it while Malcolm leaned against the door jamb and watched. He looked droopy and affected, but David did not intend to make the mistake of going over and tackling him in front of those others. He tucked himself into the shadows of another arch and waited. He knew how to wait, to relax, to let everything go slack. Patience was not just a virtue: it was an acquired technique.

After about ten minutes the banging ceased and the group began to break up. Two of the men joined Malcolm and went sauntering off down the street. Out in the daylight they showed up as youths rather than men – and could well have been part of the gang that had raided the hi-fi shop, thought David.

He could not take all of them on, all at one go. Malcolm was the prime target. Cautiously he followed them.

On the next corner the other two went their own ways, and Malcolm crossed the street into a workers' café. David took a deep breath, shoved patience back into storage, and headed for the door with its Pepsi and chocolate ads.

'Bacon roll,' Malcolm was saying. 'Double portion. Sausage, large gherkin, black coffee.'

David thought fleetingly of the herbal tea which Miss Wilmott could sometimes be persuaded to prepare for him. He was thirsty. But the smell and the steam in here did not tempt him to order a snack for himself. He waited behind Malcolm; and, instead of moving up into his place at the counter, said austerely, 'I want to talk to you about the stereo you stole.'

Malcolm spun round, his tray sliding away at an angle. As it went he snatched the mug of hot black coffee from it and threw it into David's face. It was a good job that the café did not pride itself on its scalding coffee; but the heat was still enough to sting – and enough to make David angry. He braced himself, and presented Malcolm with a perfectly timed blow in the chest. Malcolm went back, half over the counter, scattering mugs, cups, saucers, cutlery, and an assortment of sandwiches and rolls.

The girl behind the counter screamed. A door from the back opened, and someone else was yelling. Malcolm let out his own yell as David hauled him away from the wreckage and hit him again. The two of them went struggling through a confusion of tables and chairs. One table leg trapped David. Free for a second, Malcolm dashed out of the door.

Malcolm was fast, but David was faster and fitter. Malcolm could not keep up his long, loping stride. A hundred yards up the pavement, David launched himself in a rugger tackle and brought the two of them skidding to the ground. Malcolm let out a sob of defeat.

David said, 'Listen, mate. I don't like doing this, but I've got no alternative. I've got to take you somewhere.'

'No. Ain't going nowhere . . . ain't . . .'

'It's not far,' said David, hauling him up by his collar.

It was not far, but it seemed a long way when you had to drag and prod a tall, very conspicuous young West Indian along a few side streets and then a main shopping street before reaching your destination. Of the dozen or so passers-by who turned to stare, not one made a move to intervene. David was relieved, but at the same time mildly indignant that people should show so little civic spirit and ask so few questions in the interests of law and order. How did they know he wasn't a racist thug abducting a poor defenceless black?

He frog-marched the cowed Malcolm up to the front door of Mrs Chalmers's house and rang the doorbell.

'You behave yourself with this old woman,' he ordered. 'I want to be firm, but I don't want to terrify her. So speak when you're spoken to, and preferably don't speak at all.'

'Look, man—'

'It won't take a minute. But if you misbehave, I'll see it takes a lot longer – somewhere nice and quiet.'

They heard the shuffle of feet along the passage. The door opened. Mrs Chalmers peered out, saw David and then saw Malcolm, and tried to close the door again.

David shoved his right foot forward. 'Mrs Chalmers,' he said quietly, 'is this the man you saw run into the open front door of Mr Danbury's house with a stolen stereo, and run out without it?'

'It could be. I—'

'Was it?'

'Yes.'

'Well, let's telephone the police, shall we, and tell them how you made an unfortunate mistake about Mr Gray.'

Mrs Chalmers looked again from one face to the other, as if she was quite capable of changing her mind. Then she said shakily, 'You're right there. Quite right. It was just a dreadful mistake.'

Malcolm's shoulders sagged. He was too downcast to attempt even a hint of a threat to the old woman. 'All right, man, let's get it over.'

David said, 'You have a telephone, Mrs Chalmers?'

'Me? Oh, goodness gracious, no. What would I be wanting a telephone for? Hardly anyone I know left alive. And I never was one for talking a lot,' said Mrs Chalmers self-righteously.

'Never mind. I know one only a few doors away. And it would be no bad idea to wrap everything up at one go.'

In command of the situation, David led the two of them to the Danbury house. He could hear a faint clank and the movement of feet on the concrete path at the back of the building. Dale Danbury was refilling a birdbath with a watering can. He stared unwelcomingly at his three visitors.

'What do you want?'

'We're here to talk to you,' said David companionably.

'I have nothing further to say to you or your associate.'

'You owe people money,' said David, more firmly. 'It's a duty to liquidate your assets, like the car, to pay them. It's a duty, not an option. Mrs Chalmers here lied to the police about Mr Gray. She has now told me that this man ran in through the open door of your house, deposited a stolen stereo, and ran out.

Now, frankly I'm not too interested in this man himself. The hi-fi store can reclaim its stereo, the—'

'What are you talking about?'

'You want Mr Gray back. My deal includes the Mustang, includes you paying off your legitimate debt. Do you want Mr Gray, or shall we three all head off in different directions and forget it?' He kept a wary eye on Malcolm as he said it, not wanting him to take matters into his own hands.

Danbury put the watering can down with a resounding clank. He looked despairingly about his garden in search of some happier alternative.

There was none.

Two minutes later David was on the phone to the Manor office. Before an impatient Ronald King could rant on too long, he interrupted: 'It's fixed. Mrs Chalmers has gone off to the police station to retract her evidence and secure Roger's release with a statement.'

'And how is that supposed to *fix* anything?' demanded the irascible voice.

'Dale Danbury's giving us everything.'

There was a pause. When King spoke again, it was in quite a different tone. 'Log book? Letter? Permission to sell?'

'I've got the log book in front of me. He's upstairs now writing the note.'

'What's made him do it? How did *you* do it?' King sounded almost aggrieved.

'Subtlety, finesse, intellect . . . a bit of psychology. Actually,' said David, 'I feel sorry for him.'

'Yes, you would.'

David went upstairs to the little office where Danbury was seated at his desk, writing. He finished as David came in, and handed him the note. He looked disconsolate, beaten, yet calm; and at the same time deeply incensed. The gesture of handing over that note was almost an insult. Abruptly he pushed a pile of photo albums to the edge of the desk.

'You might as well have these. All the photos, the lot. Take it all. Leave me nothing. Bankrupt, broken, paupered, finished. D'you know how hard it is to make one's way in show business?

You look at me and you think, "That silly old has-been . . ." Have you any idea of the struggle, the resolve, the sacrifice, to claw your way to the top? And then to hang on for dear life, year after year, until you just run out of steam, or talent, or looks, or courage, or luck . . . or everything. And you fall. The only thing you have left is memories. I don't suppose you understand a word I've been saying?'

'I think I do,' said David.

'All I had left were memories. To you that's a rusting, rotten old motor car. To me it was my life – the pink Mustang, driving it off through the hordes of photographers to the wild weekends in big country houses . . . when I was a star!'

'Maybe one day you'll be back on top again.'

'No, I won't.' Danbury was extracting the last ounce of tragedy from the situation. 'It's all over. All I own in this whole world is a mess of old curtains, old carpets, old books . . . and my Globe Award. And shall I tell you something? Are you a betting lad?' The act was carrying him away, he was genuinely losing his temper now. 'I bet that within a month another predator creeps into this room and walks off with *that*. Oh, yes. Carries off, rips off the last item from a life in the greatest profession.' He caressed the globe held aloft by the forever petrified Hercules. 'You know it, I know it – it will *happen*!'

David spread his hands, trying to offer vague comfort; but Dale Danbury was beyond all that.

'They will come,' he asserted, challenging some evil future with his quavering chin. 'I'll be defenceless against them. You or they or someone will be back. Because it's not in the nature of carrion to leave an ounce of flesh on the corpse. You'll be back for the carpets, for the curtains, for the books, for my Award.'

'I'm sorry,' said David, genuinely.

Danbury cracked. 'Get away from me.'

There was no consolation, no soothing assurance to offer. The job was done; and David wished it could have been done less painfully. Truth and justice were truth and justice. It was just a pity that something more merciful could not be blended in with them.

'I'm sorry,' he said again. 'Really I am.'

'Get out of my house.'

Danbury was so incensed that no argument was possible. All that was left was to make a dignified exit. David was not used to the knowing, obsequious way of making oneself scarce. He backed clumsily away, reaching for the door handle and swinging himself round it towards the flight of stairs.

By the time he had reached the bottom he could hear a weird, inhuman sound from above. Either Danbury was crying hysterically, or he was churning out abuse at some unseen target. It was unnerving. Danbury's voice had already cracked into hatred and outrage. Now something else was cracking: in a terrible way he was falling apart.

David hesitated in the constricted hall, then opened the front door to let himself out.

There was a thud of footsteps on the landing above. He instinctively raised his arm above his head, fearing an attack he could not predict. Danbury, eyes wild and mouth wrenched open in a hideous, twitching grimace, was leaning over and hurling something. It was heavy, glinting, lethal. In a split second David dodged to one side, flattening himself against the wall.

The Globe Award hit the floor and bounced once. When it struck again, there was a cracking sound and it shattered into a hundred fragments.

David lowered his arm and looked up the staircase.

Danbury had gone. After the crash of the Award, the only noise was that of Dale Danbury slamming his office door. If he wept, it was alone, shut away from the world which had once fawned on him and now had utterly discarded him.

14

It would not have been David's choice of meeting place for discussing crucial legal matters. The whole ambience was characteristic of Hallday-Mostyn: a riverside pub garden with a few shrieking hoorays in one corner and a cluster of decorative but over-fluttery girls in another. It all looked summery and smart, a kind of Sloane-upon-Thames. Yet, having assembled them here, Hallday-Mostyn had chosen to withdrawn into the cool interior of the pub and chat with his cronies, leaving the awkward bit to his partner and David.

The awkward bit was Mr Hodinett.

Deirdre was spelling it patiently out to him. 'Now, Mr Hodinett, it'll be some time on the morning of the 21st. You'll be outside chambers. The court usher will invite you in, and you'll be asked fairly straightforward questions about yourself—'

'Like what, my dear?' Hodinett basked in the sunshine, oblivious to the fact that his black bowler, black suit and heavy black shoes did not really belong in this setting.

'Your name, address, and perhaps—'

'I shall be happy to oblige with those details. What I will not do is swear on the Bible. I shall affirm.'

'And please try to remember his name is David Castle, not Whittaker.'

'I'll try to remember that,' said Hodinett graciously. 'At my age, where life has accumulated such a huge trash-heap of mindless trivia, I go with the thinking of the great Voltaire – "Details are vermin".'

'Not in the Family Division, Mr Hodinett.' The sun glowed in Deirdre's hair and cast an enticing, rippling shadow across her throat and the left shoulder of her dress. 'And you do understand, we'd prefer you to *say* your character reference and not just quote from notes. It looks better.'

'What I have to say about Castle requires no *aide-memoire*. I can remember a great deal about this young man, and will inform the court accordingly.'

David shifted uneasily on the garden chair, which tilted to one side on the uneven grass. Deirdre did not look exactly enraptured by the old man's promise.

'And you'll keep it fairly brief,' she coaxed. 'Not more than five minutes.'

'Good grief. That'll hardly give me time to start my most tentative reminiscences about young James here.'

'David. David Castle.'

'Who could ever doubt it?'

David was relieved to see that Deirdre had had enough, though whether she had achieved her aim was open to doubt. Tapping a few papers together, pushing them down so that the breeze did not catch and float them gently away across the river, she said, 'Thank you very much for coming.'

Hodinett rose and smiled a benevolent smile down at the top of her head. 'It was no trouble at all. If you need me again, do endeavour to give me three days' notice by telephone.'

'But Mr Hodinett, the case is due to be heard on—'

'Good day to both of you.'

When the old man had doddered his way out of the garden, Deirdre and David sought solace inside the pub. Hallday-Mostyn was waiting, one elbow possessively on the bar. He raised a patrician eyebrow at David, inviting him to have some unspecified drink. The eyebrow, like everything else about young Hallday-Mostyn – the tie, the shirt, the lightweight suit, the cuff links – exuded self-confidence. With the case drawing ever nearer, David hoped that the confidence was justified. For himself, he did not share it.

'All buttoned up?' Hallday-Mostyn was addressing his partner.

'Oh, dear.'

'As bad as that?'

'We're going to have to see Hodinett at least one more time. He's still getting David's name wrong.'

'To be honest, I'm quite worried about Hodinett as the character witness.'

'David has no other ex-employer available to us.'

'No.' Hallday-Mostyn's tone of voice suggested that he could think of many good reasons why this should be so. 'Well, Hodinett's poor memory aside, I've now studied our case from every angle, and as far as the rest of it goes I feel growing confidence. The only complication is that where the application is so obviously just, there could be a tendency for the judge to go overboard—'

'Shifting the balance,' Deirdre took him up, 'to present all the elements *against* justice—'

'In a show of bizarre impartiality.'

David clutched the glass that had been handed to him and stared unhappily along the bar. People were talking together, someone was laughing too loudly and too long, and a young couple at a table had their heads together, murmuring, touching. They were all a million miles away from David Castle and his troubles. Worst of all, his own two supposed allies were far away. They were playing appreciatively with abstract concepts of their own. The liaison between them was that of a shared craft, an understanding which excluded poor insignificant non-professionals – like their clients.

'Now what I find significant,' Hallday-Mostyn was rambling cheerfully on, 'is that not only is our case just in itself – which is not always relevant – but that there does seem enough weight of legal possibilities to support any argument.'

'On either side, though.'

'Yes, but that adds to one's determination. It should make for quite a battle of wits.'

David might just as well not have been there. The recovery of his son was becoming simply an intellectual exercise. This was not the way he wanted his case presented before the court. Getting Sebastian for himself, instead of letting him be adopted by strangers, was the most desperate thing in his life, and that was what the judge had to be made to understand.

He looked from Deirdre to Hallday-Mostyn. They were the ones who got paid for knowing what they were doing, so you had to trust them. There was no alternative. It was their technical know-how and that of the lofty Mr Herbert Parish which would win the day.

It had to.

Even though they got paid, he thought bitterly, whichever way the verdict went.

He wished the days away, urged the court hearing to draw closer and be done with . . . to be won.

Clients seemed to be getting meaner by the day. As Ronald King walked into the office, Miss Wilmott passed him a letter delivered by hand. Nice old-fashioned way of doing things for those without enough spit to lick a stamp. Unless, of course, it was an urgent commission . . .

In which case, why had the messenger not waited for a reply?

King slit open the envelope. He began to read, then to curse. The letter-heading was as stylish and impressive as the offices of London and South Recovery Services had been. At first sight of that set-up King had vowed to climb to similar heights. There had been every sign that Mr Renton there had intended to give him a helping hand.

Now the hand was slapping him back down again.

Manor Debts had done an unquestionably satisfactory job on behalf of London and South. It had led, just as Renton had said it would, to a number of other minor commissions – minor so far as Renton's organization was concerned, but contributing very substantially to paying the rent of Manor Debt's premises. Right now King was working on details of seven individual debtors whose details had been supplied by Renton. Only right now he was told he should stop. No explanation, no complaint: just the news that London and South Recovery Services wished to dispense with the services of Manor Debt Collection Agency forthwith.

King reached for the phone.

Mr Renton was in conference. A Mr Millbray asked if he could be of any assistance. It was soon clear that he had no intention of offering any assistance whatsoever. He knew about the few small commissions which Mr King had fulfilled on Mr

Renton's behalf, but there had at no time been any formal commitment between them.

'I've recovered debts for your company well enough,' King raged. 'All on the basis of a handshake. I thought that was how you *gentlemen* worked. I've already spent a lot of time on these seven debtors you passed on to me. Why have we been dispensed with, right in the middle of it?'

'I'm sure Mr Renton has his reasons. I'm sorry you've expended any of your time. However, you did not have any contract with us. So that is the end of it.'

So far as Ronald King was concerned, it most certainly was not the end of it. He stormed out of the office, brushing aside some bleated queries from Miss Wilmott, and set off in the Rover.

The London and South receptionist tried to halt his progress, but he knew the way past her to Renton's office. Sheer impetus had got him halfway there when a doorman gave chase and put a hand on his arm.

'Sir, you have to wait in reception.'

'Not me. I'm here to see Mr Renton.'

'Reception will phone Mr Renton.'

'I can announce myself.'

The doorman tightened his grip. King twisted, shook him off, and parried a left jab. He sprinted through the inner reception office and on into the glass-walled room where Mr Renton was not what you'd call in conference – merely chatting to a subordinate.

Panting, King said, 'I want a few words with you.'

The doorman came thumping up behind him. Renton held up a placatory hand. 'All right, Claude. Just hang on there a moment.' His thin lips had almost disappeared. If he was pale, it was with cool contempt rather than fear. 'Now, Mr King, what is this extraordinary display about?'

'It's about you cancelling our arrangements.'

'What arrangements were those, Mr King?'

'We did satisfactory work for you. We've already spent time – which is money – on researches and approaches to some of these seven debtors you assigned us. Why have you turned round and told us our services are no longer required?'

161

Renton's voice was level and impassive. 'This is a very cut-and-thrust business, Mr King. When I look for a service I go to the people who provide it at the time I want it, and provide the best.'

'Ours is the best.'

'You did some quite commendable routine work for us. Now we've found someone we're better suited with.'

'And who would that be?'

'A new company, just started up. Right on your doorstep, oddly enough.' Renton appeared to find this mildly, ironically amusing. 'Very good at the job. Much more efficient than you, as a matter of fact. They waste no time.'

'I don't believe you.'

'I gave you seven debtors three weeks ago. We've heard nothing from you. Our new colleagues have persuaded two to pay up already.'

'Which two? And who *are* these new boys?'

'It is a confidential matter whom we employ. We're only interested in results, Mr King, and you don't produce them as fast as these other people.'

This time Renton offered the doorman a nod instead of a halt sign. King went quietly.

He was not so quiet by the time he got back to the office. Miss Wilmott looked up, opened her mouth, closed it again, and kept her head well down.

'Where's David?'

'You know it's his day in court, Mr King.'

Of course. It would be. Big day for David Castle – and just when he was most needed right here. A day when King really needed him, and he had gone missing. And heaven only knew what state he would be in when he did get back.

Really, there just wasn't any justice in the world.

David sat in an inhospitable corridor staring at the darkly gleaming hair of the girl who had been so close and was now such a stranger, surrounded by strangers. The thickset man, uncomfortable in a business suit when he ought surely to have been in tweeds, must be Anne's brother. Others in her group were unidentifiable.

And who was David Castle to have doubts about the man's attire, when he felt such a stranger in his own cramping suit? He tugged at the flap of a pocket; eased his neck and hoped he would not develop a sudden irresistible itch.

Deirdre came up beside him. 'Is that her?'

'Yes.'

'She's pretty.'

'Not to me.'

'Don't radiate gloom and despondency.'

'Why shouldn't I? Everything's out of my control now. Nothing I can cope with.'

'We're going to win.'

Along the hall came the figures of Hallday-Mostyn and Parish, more confident and mutually congratulatory than ever in their familiar surroundings. They boomed their good mornings, spared a fleeting glance for David's suit and general appearance, and looked as finely poised as actors awaiting their cue. When the doors into the courtroom opened they swept in, settled themselves, distributed their papers and law books, and rose gracefully when the judge entered.

And so to the matter of Sebastian Merton, a minor.

Sebastian was not even present. Whatever was to be accomplished on his behalf, he would have no say in the matter. There was no need for the key figure in this whole charade even to appear on the actual scene.

Parish cleared his throat and smiled, managing to combine deference and complacency in equal proportions.

'My Lord, I appear for the applicant in this action, and my learned friend Mr Horace Chilton appears for the respondent.' There was a ritual exchange of courteous nods. 'My Lord, this is an action for custody of a minor, Sebastian Merton, under the Guardianship of Minors' Act. The applicant is the father of the child born on the seventh of April 1982. The child is illegitimate and now lives with his mother. The father, David Castle, lives alone. He has an excellent career with equally excellent prospects. His relationship with the mother broke up seven months before the child was born. It is the nature of that relationship and how the mother chose to terminate it which forms the basis of our arguments for custody.'

David found himself staring again at Anne. She caught his gaze and looked away with a slight wriggle of distaste. He remembered that pouting expression all too well: it could be deliciously provocative or peevish and dismissive, and right now it was dismissive. She did not want to be in this courtroom. She didn't have the patience for this sort of thing. The sooner it was over and she could get away, the better pleased she would be. David felt the same, provided the result was the one he wanted.

Something clutched at his stomach. The sight of Anne, the thought of Sebastian, the whole sour atmosphere of the situation and this place twisted at his guts. He doubled up, racked by acid indigestion. That rice bread he had eaten for breakfast was probably not helping. He must have had too much, eating compulsively without noticing. But if he hadn't eaten at all, then his stomach would almost certainly have rumbled too loudly for these hallowed surroundings. Did stomach gurglings and rumblings count as contempt of court?

Deirdre looked apprehensively at him as he bent forward and stayed that way.

Parish was orating on. 'The evidence we shall produce will support an argument that in essence is quite simple and irrefutable. Miss Anne Merton has not to this day contested that on announcing to Mr Castle that she was pregnant, he immediately offered marriage. She cannot deny that this prospective marriage was discussed and there was talk of a September wedding in the local family church near Chalfont St Giles. Then in mid-August Miss Merton informed Mr Castle that she had changed her mind and would not marry him. That is part one of the narrative. Part two of the evidence which we shall produce shows that Miss Merton has deliberately contrived over the past two years to keep this father from seeing his child – which of course may now appear to favour her case on the basis of the "continuity of care" principle . . .'

His theorizing faded into infinity as David tried to cope with the repetitive stabbing pains. He found the strength to whisper to Deirdre: 'Can I leave the court . . . get some Rennies . . .?'

'No, you can't. What on earth's the matter?'

'I ate something indigestible this morning.'

'You know, David, quite a few things about you are indigestible,' she whispered ferociously.

He tried to sit up straight.

'Justice,' Parish was saying at full, resonant volume. 'That is what we insist must be seen to be done on this very simple issue. Miss Merton became pregnant. Mr Castle offered marriage. Marriage details were planned. Mr Castle behaved honourably throughout. It was Miss Merton who without reasonable cause changed her mind. Now Miss Merton has indulged in another change of mind. The child whom she failed to legitimize by accepting the father's proposal, she now wishes to discard and hand over to her brother.'

David tried to concentrate, but all his attention was held by the pain. Often in the past when he was nervous he had suffered attacks of bowel colic. This one was a stunner of its kind. When the time came, he was not sure that he would be able to stand upright and make the good impression on the court that was essential.

Parish was concluding his peroration. 'Mr Castle, the natural father, who has the will, the means, and the heartfelt desire to bring up his child, will be strongly contesting any attempt at an adoption order.' He turned encouragingly and commandingly. 'I would now like to call upon Mr David Castle.'

15

The scrapyard resembled an abstract sculpture in twisted
metal and tottering towers of convoluted piping. Ronald King,
however, was not used to seeing things in the abstract. To him
this was a down-at-heel tip whose owner had precious few
assets with which to pay off his debts. Yet still those debts had
to be paid. King had called here once before and met only with
excuses. This time, even though he was theoretically no longer
in Renton's employ, he wanted more.

O'Rourke, clambering over a pile of guttering, saw King and
groaned, but came down from his precarious perch.

'I called on you five days ago about your debts, Mr
O'Rourke.'

'I know you did.'

'I just wondered if you could help me.' O'Rourke's grimly
suspicious stare suggested that he was trying to work out what
sort of veiled threat this might be. 'Has anybody been here
since then,' asked King, 'to discuss the money you owe?'

'No one but you.'

'Well, you want to watch it. Apparently there's a bunch of
heavy con men making the rounds, saying they're collecting
debts. If they turn up, would you call me? I'll sort them out, that
I promise you.'

He handed O'Rourke his card. O'Rourke accepted it with ill
grace and went on looking as if he still wondered what the
catch was.

Another of the seven debtors was in business not more than
five minutes' drive away. King chose him as second on the list
for investigation.

Even as he drew up, he could guess what the outcome of this
enquiry would be. Outside the office of Fielding's Estate

Agency an Alfa Romeo lying on its side was being carefully turned over and winched up on to a recovery truck. The main plate-glass window of the office itself had been shattered, and two men were hammering large sheets of hardboard into place.

King picked his way over shards of broken glass which had been summarily swept into the gutter. Inside, an angle-poise lamp on Fielding's desk fought off the gloom within the boarded-up window.

'Mr Fielding, last week we discussed your bookmaker debts—'

'Which I told you were a bloody stupid error on the part of the man's bloody stupid assistant.'

'I just wondered if anybody else had been in to see you since.'

'You could say that,' said Fielding rancorously. He pushed a business card across the desk.

King studied it. Hercules Debt Recovery, 22 Barnes New Road. Yes, that was very much his patch.

'They broke the window,' said Fielding, 'and overturned my car. And they said they'd be back.'

'How many?'

'Four big ones.'

'Have you called the police?'

'That would be a terrific idea. If we had a halfway proper police force you wouldn't *have* hooligans like that roaming the streets terrorizing people.'

It was not a point on which King felt himself qualified to argue.

The address on the card led him to the premises of a minicab firm, with a small concrete apron in front of it. Two drivers were cleaning their windscreens as he tucked the Rover into the extreme end of the lot. They glanced at him but raised no objection as he left the Rover and paced round the building until he found a side door with a cheap new plastic sign on it. The sign announced that this was the registered office of Hercules Debt Recovery.

Inside it looked cheap and tatty. The office was squalid, the window small and not too clean. Like Fielding, four men were making do with a desk lamp. It was focused not on work but on a table on to which one of them had just thrown three playing cards.

King said, 'Good morning. I'm looking for Hercules Debt Recovery.'

The smallest of the men looked up. He was small only in comparison with the others, and there was a heavy menace in his flushed face under its mop of sandy hair.

'You've found it.'

'My name is Ronald King, Manor Debt Collection.' He flipped his own card on to the table beside the deck already there. 'Your company's new to this area. We've been here quite a while.'

'So?'

'So we're a little surprised to find you turning up, as it were, right on our doorstep, Mr . . . er . . .?'

'Stimson. Not that knowing it'll make any difference. What d'you want?'

'I'd like to be frank with you, Mr Stimson. A company called London and South Recovery, whom we've done good work for, recently gave us seven debtors to collect from. This morning the operation has been taken away from us and turned over to you.'

The men had stopped playing, but three of them kept mutely studying the cards in their hands. Stimson laid his cards face down on the table and said, 'I don't know anything about that.'

'Two debt recovery companies in business less than a mile and a half away from each other – well, I think we should enter into meaningful discussions, or else at some point we're liable to get in each other's hair.'

'No one's going to get in our hair, Mr King.' Stimson jerked his shock of hair at the other three, who, still without uttering a word, got up and went out of the office.

King decided it was time to get tough. 'You've taken London Recovery's business away from us. I don't like that. And you seem to get your results by smashing up property – Fielding's window, damage to his car . . . what's next? You do that, the constabulary is going to be banging on both our doors. I have a nice little business in this area and I'm here to tell you that you're not going to screw it up.'

'Is that it?'

'Yes.'

Stimson stared him out. 'Go away.'

'I'll go. But just let's get it clear. I am not going to let you ruin my business.'

When King emerged into the street, the two minicab drivers had gone. Nor was there any sign of Stimson's three associates. But there was ample sign that they had a limited repertoire of meaningful gestures: King's Rover had been tipped over on its side on the concrete apron, in similar fashion to Fielding's Alfa Romeo.

King spun round and flung his way back into the office. Stimson, like the rest of them, had gone. They all stayed out of sight while King called the only garage proprietor he had ever trusted – and then only because he knew enough about him to have him put away several times over. King had learned long ago that there were only three kinds of garage owners or managers: those who were incompetent, those who were dishonest, and those who were both incompetent and dishonest. Even Mike Ilkley had to be stood over the whole time. But used as he was to being stood over, even Ilkley did not feel that he had to add politeness to his subservience. When he had come out and helped to get the Rover back on to its four wheels, and they had driven back to the garage to inspect the buckled side, he said, 'I'll never understand why you've lavished so much monies on an old banger like this.'

'This isn't an old banger. It's a classic motor vehicle.' Once again he thought of Dale Danbury, and recalled the deal over the pink Mustang. 'A collector's item.'

'It's a self-defeating exercise.'

'Just quote me a price before you've thought up a con for doubling it.'

'You're looking at the wrong end of six hundred.'

'*You're* looking at it. I'm looking round to see who's the mug you think you're talking to.'

Ilkley ran a finger along the roof. 'This is a ripple. You might have chassis crease.'

'Five hundred,' said King. 'I'll bring it in on Friday morning. And don't knock it – and I mean don't knock it with your tongue or any other damn thing. And now,' he said darkly, 'I've got a bit of a problem.'

Ilkley's wary leer implied that this would not be the first time and that he was not all that keen on being involved in any problems beyond those concerning repairs to a motor car.

'Four blokes,' said King. 'Large blokes, bad, making trouble. I was thinking of your drinking pals – the O'Connor brothers and Billy Mason.'

'That sort of trouble.'

'Yes, that sort.'

'You want these four large blokes to experience stress?'

'They leave me no alternative.'

'That'll cost you more than donks out and paintwork on this motor.'

'Yeah.'

'I'll check it out,' said Ilkley. 'Give me a tinkle later.'

'I'll do that.' King slid back into the car and gingerly pulled the door shut. 'And I won't be leaving it all that much later, so get busy.'

'You were nicer when you were just a vicious policeman,' said Ilkley.

King ignored this parting shot and drove off.

The buckled side of the Rover kept squeaking every time he slowed down. It let out a particularly repulsive whine when King drew to a halt outside the Manor Debt premises. It was not the only one. As soon as he opened the outer door of the office he could hear Miss Wilmott sobbing and whining. She was collapsed across the chair behind her desk, hiccuping with sobs and little shrieking intakes of breath.

'What happened?'

But, as with his first sight of Fielding's office, he already knew. There had of course been four men, and he could almost have reeled off a description of them without waiting for Miss Wilmott's stumbling account. They had thrown her aside, told her what they would do to her if she uttered another sound, and gone on into King's office to take it apart. The filing cabinets were over on their sides with the drawers tugged open and papers scattered all over the floor. His desk was upside down. His chair had been dismembered.

'I phoned the police.' Miss Wilmott was shivering in the doorway.

'And?'

'I suppose they're on their way.'

King longed to slump down into a chair and get his breath back, but there was no chair available any longer. 'Any word from David's lawyer about when they expect to be finished?'

'No.'

'Still at it?' King thumped his fist against the open door. 'I need him *here*. Our entire livelihood threatened, while he . . .*him*, he's in court arguing about a bastard. As if we didn't have enough bastards on our hands already!'

Mr Chilton's opening address and cross-examination were suave and insinuating. There was nothing in any specific sentence to which anyone could take exception; but his manner was calculated to pull rugs slyly from under any witness's feet and leave him teetering off balance.

'The best interests of the child, Mr Castle. That is what we are here to debate this morning. The child foremost and exclusively. But before we get to the child we must discuss prior motive. And I think we must deal with and dismiss the canard of the offer spurned. Let us not have any over-emphasis on the proposed plans for the little church outside Chalfont St Giles. I have come to the conclusion, Mr Castle, that a large part of your argument is that your offer of marriage to a pregnant lady somehow squares everything and puts you in the right. It has been made to sound very moral, very righteous. I don't think that it is. I have an old-fashioned view of rights and wrongs, Mr Castle, and I believe that the offer of marriage should come *before* the pregnancy.'

David, standing groggily on his feet and trying not to wince too noticeably at each repeated stab in his stomach, was aware of Deirdre and Hallday-Mostyn frowning and whispering together.

'That said, can we now dismiss this issue from all our minds?' continued the opposition barrister. 'Marriage offers repudiated have nothing to do with our main concern at this

moment. That concern is with the best interest of the child –
you'll agree, Mr Castle?'

'Is that some kind of a question?'

'I beg your pardon?' said Chilton silkily.

'I though this was supposed to be a cross-examination. I
thought you wanted to know the real truth, but you haven't
asked me what I'd call one real question . . .'

'Oh, I have plenty of questions. Questions about the best
interests of the child. Please be patient. All in good time. Let's
talk first about how your son has been brought up by Miss
Merton, and what unceasing and generous help she has had
from her brother, who now hopes to proceed to adopt your son
and bring him up in a style becoming . . .'

He droned on. Some of the drone was directed at last into
the form of cunningly contemptuous questions to which David
could return only those same old answers, in the same old
words, reciting the same depressing facts which he had gone
over so many wearisome times with Deirdre and Mr Herbert
Parish. Mr Parish, he noted, appeared at this moment to be
either asleep or utterly lost in a daydream of faraway pleasures.

Just about the time when David was afraid he was about to be
sick all over his neatly pressed suit, the questioning ended and
he was allowed to sit down. He could barely grasp where it had
all led. He looked at Deirdre for reassurance. She looked
incapable of offering it.

A Miss Bird was summoned to the witness stand. Now Mr
Chilton discarded his insidious sneer and became kind and
respectful. For her part, Miss Bird had clearly been well
rehearsed and spoke crisply and competently, making it plain
that she was not a woman whose words should be taken lightly,
and certainly never dismissed lightly.

'I have made over twenty official visits to see Mrs Merton
and her son as a social worker, and several unofficial visits
because I liked Miss Merton and her little boy. On many
occasions when visiting the household I have met Mr George
Merton and his wife. They are a childless couple, but I think
anyone would be greatly touched by the way in which they look
after little Seb when mother has to be away as part of her work

as an exhibition demonstrator. I offer my considered opinon that Mr and Mrs Merton would make excellent prospective adopters for Seb.'

Deirdre leaned closer to David. 'Social workers! I've never met one I've liked. All worse than useless. Half the social problems of this country would diminish tomorrow if they were all fired.'

David was indignant. 'What a terrible attitude to take! You can't make sweeping condemnations about people who are trying to do some good.'

'You do realize that she's not on *your* side?'

'That doesn't mean she's not doing her best as she sees it to—'

'You can either make sweeping condemnations,' Deirdre hissed, 'or you can lead a life with your head in a bucket of sand. Take your choice.'

They glared at each other, antagonists rather than allies.

'Thank you, Miss Bird,' said Chilton benignly, making way for Herbert Parish.

Parish opened his eyes and stood up. Parish would never double up with indigestion or show any likelihood of falling over. 'Miss Bird, as a social worker in multiple contact with Miss Merton, can you tell me, did she ever discuss the child's natural father with you?'

'I don't think . . . that is, I gathered she didn't like to discuss him, outside just giving me the barest details for my notes.'

'And what about you? Did you ever advance the theory that the boy might benefit from having a natural father around?'

'I got the impression she didn't like the natural father. Didn't like him at all.'

David winced. The judge leaned forward a fraction to study him coldly and analytically.

'So, would you agree,' Parish persevered, 'that the picture we're getting supports the proposition that the interests of the child are thought best served by Miss Merton turning down a sincere offer of marriage, not talking to the child about his father, and refusing the father access to him? Is that correct?'

'I'm not sure I can comment generally. The child seems very happy.'

'Would it not be truer to say the child may be happy in the only world he has been allowed to know, which is the world of his mother's decisions?'

Chilton was on his feet. 'My Lord, I object. My learned friend is leading the witness.'

'Yes, Mr Parish. Please rephrase your question.'

David sank down in his uncomfortable seat. None of this weaving and dancing and play-acting had anything to do with what he felt about Sebastian and what he wanted for Sebastian himself. He was dazed by their incomprehension. Parish was not getting to the core of it. Nobody was.

During the lunch recess he and Deirdre went down to a pub on the Embankment. He could have done without food or drink. Push the case through, be done with it: who could possibly want an interval for food and chit-chat at this stage?

He was glad that Hallday-Mostyn had not joined them. And Mr Parish would of course never have deigned to. Yet at the same time, if Hallday-Mostyn had chosen not to show his face, did that mean that he was ashamed, or scared of having to give an honest opinion of the way things were going so far?

Deirdre was trying to make conversation. He replied automatically, but what he tried to say came out even more muddled than the speeches in court, and another part of his brain was conjuring up different visions.

How could she even begin to understand? Once or twice he had tried to explain aikido principles to her, so that she might grasp some of the motives that moved him and gave him hope. She had listened earnestly and asked polite questions, but he knew that to her the whole concept could never be anything but foreign and eccentric. Right at this moment she could not even guess at his inner despair.

Beliefs were slipping away. Or else they were taking a new and unforeseen shape.

What David had never told her was that during a five-year period of his life he had read every book on Buddhism and Zen Buddhism he could lay his hands on. And in Java, on a naval 'show the flag' good-will visit, he had once been able to sit for hours at the feet of a guru – a wonderful man whose spiritual strength he wished he could call on right now. Aikido was a self-defence which turned the force of an enemy's attack against that enemy. But more important, it was a totally enveloping Buddhist philosophy, based on and illuminated by the concept of passive resistance. That was what David had been striving to live all these years – Buddhist passivity. Only now, in the middle of this grotesque court case, he could no longer be passive. He was totally, emotionally, actively angry. Which meant that he had lost all the terms of reference of the way he had been living these last eight years.

'I think you'd better know it,' he said aloud, to her bewilderment: 'I think I'm totally screwed up.'

Back in court, Parish called Mr Hodinett. It was Hodinett's big moment, and he looked in a mood to savour it to the full.

'I was quite happy to give a character reference concerning this young man David,' he said at a stately pace, 'though it's no easy task. I'm now of the age when we are talking about not one but several generations. Several generations between myself and this young man. However, he's a fine feller. Conscientious, responsible, intelligent.'

Deirdre breathed a faint sigh of relief. Now wrap it up neatly – David could sense her silent urging – and sit down.

But Hodinett was getting into his stride. 'I was extremely happy to employ him for all the time he was with my firm – eleven months exactly. I'm sorry for all the troubles he has had, much of which I'm sure he is innocent of, except in his poor relations with the Fates, though perhaps he is not entirely blameless. As the good Ovid said, *Si quoties homines peccant, sua fulmina mittat, Jupiter, exiguo tempore inermis erat.*'

Parish was delighted to translate for the benefit of those who had forgotten their Latin. 'If Jupiter threw a thunderbolt for every sin man commits, soon he would have none to throw.'

'Exactly.' Hodinett beamed approval.

'But now, Mr Hodinett—'

'As to Whittaker's background, I know many of his family. Again I fall between the generations of his father and grandfather. I remember well the grandfather, Rear Admiral Whittaker – "Cormorant Dick", as they called him after Jutland. I'm not sure how many of those present here will recall that epic story. Dick Whittaker went after the original *Graf Spee* in pea-soup fog and trounced the wretched Hunnish matelots, sending down to Davy Jones's locker, if my memory serves me, no less than Grand Admiral Speidel . . .'

'May I interrupt one second, my Lord?' Chilton was looking very smug. 'The character witness is referring to a family by the name of Whittaker. The applicant is named Castle.'

The judge nodded. 'Mr Hodinett?'

'My sincere apologies. An unpardonable mistake. Age shall not weary us, but it plays a certain havoc with one's specific recollections of names. However' – he pointed at David – 'that is the man I know, and I recommend to all of you as an honest, upright citizen and a fine lad. Is that enough?'

'Yes,' said Parish briskly. 'Thank you, Mr Hodinett.'

It dragged on. Mr George Merton was briefly questioned, largely on financial matters and the number of rooms and bathrooms in his house. Anne Merton spoke of her concern that Sebastian should have the best opportunities in life, and made it clear that from the start she had known David Castle would be incapable of providing these.

Then Parish was up again. 'I refer, my Lord, to R.V. Oxford City Justices, ex parte H.'

A large book was carried to the bench by the usher, who opened it at the appropriate page. The judge silently thanked him, and after glancing down the page returned his attention to Parish.

'Yes?'

'This was a case in respect of an illegitimate child in care on the ground that the child's mother, who suffered mental illness, was incapable of caring for the child. The putative father sought to issue a complaint under the relevant sections of the Guardianship of Minors Act 1971 that the custody of the child be committed to him . . .'

David tapped Hallday-Mostyn on the shoulder. 'I don't know what's going on here.'

'I think we're just trying a couple of wingers.'

'What is there to wing? There's enough to back our case up without a lot of stuff about Anne being bonkers. I don't see the point.'

The judge appeared to be having the same difficulty. Leaning forward again, he said, 'One moment, please. Are you suggesting that there is evidence or that you will produce evidence of mental illness in this mother?'

'Mental illness is subject to wide definition. We have submitted our independent social worker's report, and there is clear concern in it about this mother's alienation, perhaps self-evident in her wish not to bring up her child but to farm it out to adoption.'

The judge brooded over this for a few moments, then closed the book in front of him. 'I think we are raising another canard here, Mr Parish. I believe we would be on firmer ground with the *ratio decidenda* of the decision of the Divisional Court' – he tapped the cover of the book of law reports – 'to be found in a passage at the end of the judgment of Payne T., after referring to a decision in re M, Court of Appeal . . .'

David's stomach-ache had gone. Now he had a splitting headache. There was no way of dealing with this onrush of nonsense. Mental illness, references and cross-references, verbal sparring – this had nothing to do with him trying to get his son back from a mother who didn't want him.

His head throbbed more and more excruciatingly. He ceased to hear the words, ceased to see anything around him.

Not a month had passed since the birth of his son when he had not tried to contact Anne, sometimes by phone but mostly by letter, because she would not come to the phone. He had won access only seven times all told, and those mainly around Christmas and the boy's birthday. On most occasions he had to admit his approach had been almost threatening: he would phone from near the house, telling Anne's mother that he was just going to drop in. But as a matter of policy he had been kept away from Sebastian as firmly as possible. Now, in this court, through the haze of agony, he was beginning to realize why. He had been calculatingly made a stranger to his son by the mother because she had always had a custody battle like this in her mind.

'It's a farce,' he said out loud.

'Bad luck, old man. I'm sorry.' In the corridor outside the court, Parish was patting his shoulder paternally. And then Parish and

Hallday-Mostyn were heading away, chatting about some of the more amusing incidents in the case.

Deirdre touched David's arm. It remained stiff and unresponsive.

'David, I'm so sorry. Look, I'm going to go after Mr Parish. We'll have a quick chat about leave to appeal.'

'You do that,' he heard himself saying.

'I'll see you later.'

'No.'

'What d'you mean?'

'I don't want to see you later. I'd like to be on my own. I'll phone you in a few days.'

Her eyes looked bruised. 'I don't think you should take it like this.'

She didn't? He had lost his son. Everything that had happened in that court had been a total travesty of justice.

Deirdre went off after Parish and Hallday-Mostyn. He watched her go, but somehow without seeing her. He was still there, incapable of moving or making any kind of decision, when doors swung open and Anne came through. A solicitor and Mr Horace Chilton flanked her, talking brightly in mutual approval. As they passed him, David found his voice again.

'Excuse me.'

Ann turned and looked. Her face did not alter.

'Give my love to my child,' said David.

The three of them quickened their pace and moved away up the corridor.

16

'Well, well, Ronald,' said Detective Chief Inspector Caley in gloating commiseration, 'they do seem to have given you a going-over, don't they?'

King sat in the CID Sierra beside Caley and tried not to react too aggressively. Right now he knew that he needed Caley's back-up for the rough vengeance he had in mind.

'On *your* Manor,' he said. 'Not the sort of thing you want to overlook, is it? Unless there's an . . . arrangement.'

'No. There is not an arrangement. So let's be hearing your side of it.'

'A group of four. Call themselves Hercules Debt Recovery. Their operation is recovering debts fast – by beating people up.'

'That's usually considered a bit previous down our nick. Though some of our oppos have had this reputation of being a little heavy-handed, as you'll remember, Ronald.'

King said stolidly, 'We were on the side of the law.'

'Now you mention it, I suppose we were.' Caley grinned to himself, not really inviting anyone to share it.

King handed over a typed sheet. It was the list of the seven debtors who had once been in his province but had since been extradited by his rivals. He explained the situation round at the estate agency, and indicated O'Rourke's name. They hadn't got round to O'Rourke yet, but he was in the firing line. The assault could come any day now, any hour.

'There's a good collar in this,' he said, 'and I'll help with evidence.'

'I'll look into it.'

'I want them well and truly lumbered. Then we can share out a few . . . well, reminiscences.'

'Pity you're not still in the Met,' said Caley. 'A sad reflection on the Force that a villain like you feels he has no place in it any longer.' He waited until King was out on the pavement, then leaned over and looked upward. 'But it might get me that way, one day, just the way it got you. So I'll watch over your interests. Manor Debt may be a great big skyscraper block one day, right? And you'll have plum jobs on offer.'

This time they both exchanged genuine grins. A lot more dependable in their crooked way, thought King, than a handshake from the likes of Renton.

He went off to see Mike Ilkley again. Ilkley allowed himself another brief inspection of the Rover's scarred side and wrinkled his nose as if wondering whether to recommend O'Rourke's scrapyard. Instead he muttered, 'They're on. O'Connor brothers and Billy Mason.'

'Nice. What you might call carrying some weight.'

'One hundred smacks a day each. Then when we deliver the punch, that's an extra five.'

'You must be joking?'

'Only if the City pages of the *Sun* are joking, man. It's called hyper-inflation.'

'In my book it's called something quite different.'

'Yes or no?'

'Yes,' growled King. 'Right then, let's have results. I gave you the Hercules address.'

'Yep.'

'Four outsize blokes. Their top man's called Stimson. Thatch of gingery hair that needs some salt rubbing into it. Can't mistake 'em. So when'll you be starting?'

Ilkley spared the Rover another glance, then averted his eyes. 'Well, there's no paint jobs really pressing. Maybe now.'

'Thanks.'

King drove off. He felt a tingle of anticipation. It was all going to happen. With Caley on the move as well as Ilkley and his mates, something should descend quite heavily on the Stimson stable before too long. Even Hercules would get some pains in his shoulders from this little lot. King only wished he could be present when the first blow fell.

Late that afternoon he wished even more fervently that he had been around. Things could not possibly have got so madly out of hand if he had been there.

It was O'Rourke who filled in the details.

He had been cutting up some old sheets of zinc with an acetylene flame when Stimson and another man of about the same height and considerably more breadth came across the yard. The man in charge had to be Stimson: O'Rourke's description of him to King tallied perfectly.

'You owe Jack Hanlon the money-lender six grand,' said Stimson. 'We're here to collect it.'

O'Rourke admitted to King that, whatever his first impressions might have been, he would now have preferred to deal with Manor rather than Hercules, and that if he could have got close enough to the phone to ring King, as advised, he would have done just that. But the two men were not going to let him anywhere near a phone. Stimson's companion grabbed and held him while Stimson snatched the flaming acetylene gun away. Flame brushed along the metal of the oxygen cylinder.

'Ever seen the explosion when a welding torch is left touching an oxygen cylinder?'

'You're mad.'

'It'd just about level this yard, I reckon. I'll give you a demo next time we visit and you still haven't got the money for Jack Hanlon.'

To O'Rourke it had looked for a few seconds as if Stimson wanted to do something nasty and destructive right there and then. But the other man had let go of O'Rourke and was peering through the rusting mesh of the fence.

'We're being tailed. Four monkeys.'

'Next week, then,' said Stimson. And he and his sidekick made a sprint for the back doors, out down the lane and away.

'Only I don't know if they made it,' O'Rourke told King. 'There was a lot of yelling, and I'll swear that was a police car out front – you know, plain clothes and plain vehicle – and there was four blokes running like mad and then splitting up. . . .'

'I thought you told me only two came and leaned on you.'

'Straight up it was only two. But I swear there was four outside there, and that car, and somebody was having one hell of a punch-up.'

Obviously, thought King in a generous fit of tolerance, poor old O'Rourke had gone a bit groggy after the experience of Stimson and his gorilla. It was hard to blame him. In such circumstances he could hardly expect to be taken as a reliable witness.

'But what gets me,' said O'Rourke, 'is where the police went afterwards. I mean, if it *was* police, and they *were* wheeling that lot off to the nick, why didn't they come and ask me what happened? If there were two others outside, and they were hanging about and then the other two showed up, or if . . .' He gave up.

'Let me go and make a few discreet enquiries,' suggested King.

'Oh, great. And while you're away, suppose they're let out and come back and take it all out on me?'

'Why should they be let out that fast?' asked King reasonably.

Only when he had made the twitching O'Rourke see reason did he drive round to the station to catch up with the good tidings.

DCI Caley looked just as smug as King felt. 'Two out of four,' he said. 'The other two were too quick for us.'

'Two's not bad. The message ought to get through.'

'One snag is, we're going to have to frame this charge a bit carefully. I mean, you know in your bones when someone's loitering with intent, but it can be difficult to prove that intent in court.'

'Loitering? They weren't loitering. Two of 'em were right inside, threatening a scorched earth policy right across O'Rourke's premises.'

'All four were outside,' said Caley flatly.

'After the heavies had left, they were, but you go round and ask O'Rourke—'

'They were outside,' said Caley, 'on their way in. Looked as if they'd spotted someone going in and were on their heels. If you're saying there were already two inside, that makes six.'

King felt an ominous chill. None of this was adding up the way he had calculated.

Caley had acquired a querulous frown. 'Another snag. Seems a bit of a rum do to me. I wouldn't want you to be leading me up some garden path, Ronald, but somebody does seem to have got somebody's knickers in a twist.'

'What the hell d'you mean?'

'I'm not sure. Either someone's trying to set you up, or . . . Look, one of those we've got says he's never worked for Hercules Debt Recovery. His name's Ilkley. He says he's employed by *you*.'

The terrible truth dawned on Ronald King. 'Oh, God,' he breathed.

Caley was waiting for an explanation.

'So there we are,' said King. He looked despondently round the sitting room of David's flat and reached again for the whisky bottle. 'Or rather, here we are.'

David let himself sink into the couch. He would have been happy to let it engulf him, suffocate him. He did not take the glass King was holding out to him, but lacked the strength to wave it away. King put it down on the rickety little coffee table.

'So my gallant bloody troops rush off to collar the Hercules heavies' – King swilled a mouthful back – 'and get collared themselves. I suppose that's what comes of playing both ends against the middle – and then getting caught in the middle.'

'I've had enough,' said David. 'It stinks. All of it.'

'So the first hint of real bother we get into, you're off.'

'I didn't say I was off.'

'Then what are we going to do about it? I think I'm saying, what are *you* going to do about it? I know it's my business, but you're an integral part of it.' When there was no reply, his hectoring tone softened. 'Okay, I do understand. You're all upset at the moment. I . . . oh, I'm sorry. Very sorry. And sorry you seem to have had a splat with your Deirdre.'

This got through to David. He had tried to push the past and all thoughts of Sebastian aside, and think about the future and where Deirdre fitted into it and what he was going to say when he got round to phoning her. But it was all too soon.

Only how did King know or guess there had been a cooling off?

King explained. 'I had to phone her. For business reasons.

The moment I got back here. I mean, she's got to do something about Billy Mason and Ilkley getting arrested, saying they were working for me. What a mess!' After a moment's reflection he began to sound stroppy again. 'Can't you say something? I mean, you *are* an employee of mine.'

David was almost too washed out to bother replying. All he could manage was: 'I don't need the job any more. I was only working for money to pay lawyers.' This time he waved the drink away as King prodded it across the table.

'Look, you've lost your boy. You got troubles. I got troubles. Let's treat it like a tragedy. I mean if my cousin walked in here and said, "Ronald, your old mum's dead," I mean, first thing he'd hand me a whisky. Or a brandy. So—'

'You told me you didn't know your mother. You were brought up by an aunt.'

'So it's my aunt who's died.'

'Long before your uncle,' said David pedantically. 'It was your uncle who left you that money, remember? That's how we met.'

'So it was.' King refilled his own glass. 'I know you don't rate me too high as a thinker, or a friend . . .'

David was stung. He decided to pick up the drink after all, and its fiery warmth stirred up another flickering warmth, the first he had felt all day. 'I do rate you,' he protested. 'You've been very good to me. You've always been straight with me.'

King, embarrassed, raised his glass. They both drank.

And went on drinking. There was really little else for them to do at this stage, at this hour of the night . . . and on into the small hours of the morning. Several times David made the effort to pull himself together and think coherently about the future; but the past kept intruding, and to lull the pain of it he did not protest when King kept replenishing his glass.

He was still stunned, and might as well stay that way. Somehow he had never expected that verdict. It was the whole idea of that enormous, imposing edifice of law, without a suggestion of a crack or a fault in its structure, this bastion of righteousness – within whose courts, in the end, everything added up to just a load of rubbish . . . He couldn't have his own son, because a girl was going to give him to her brother because he had more money. And Deirdre wasn't separate from the madness, she was part of it. He could not let himself be anything in the life of someone who was part of *that* sort of life.

If she were sitting here right now, he would tell her so.

If she were sitting here right now . . .

King, slurred and maudlin, spluttered suddenly: 'I'm ruined. Ruined.'

David forced himself to put his glass down. He sat upright and tried to persuade the room to stop shifting about. King's face, from this angle, was as blurred as his voice. But something clear was emerging into David's mind. Things stopped swaying, and stabilized around it.

'You're not,' he said firmly. 'You're not ruined. All it is, you've been attacked by a force. I'll help you take that force and use it against the initiators.'

'Help yourself,' said King muzzily.

'That's something I can win at. I can't win at law because I'm too subjective, but I can win with my aikido. I'm telling you . . .'

But there was no point in telling King anything for a while. He had slumped down into his chair and was sound asleep. Weary, but with a strange, mystical new confidence, David headed towards the bedroom and passed out without even getting as far as taking his shoes off.

In the morning he had a cold bath and did a few limbering up exercises. King groaned and tried not to look. King was also reluctant to go out into the daylight, but David's bleak determination carried him along with it.

It carried them both to O'Rourke's scrapyard, where O'Rourke was prepared to go over the events of the previous day once more.

'He took this cutter, see, and brushed it up and down the cylinder.' He demonstrated with the flame from the oxy-acetylene cutter in his hand, gingerly flicking it along the cylinder. 'I tell you, if he'd held the flame up against the cylinder directly for half a minute, it'd explode. We'd be badly burned for sure – might level the yard, like he said.'

'But he'd be mad to do it himself,' said David. 'Not much of a threat, if you know he wouldn't dare carry it out.'

'Sods like that give you the big warning,' said King, 'and then work out the ways of fulfilling it without getting their own necks too close.'

'That I understand. Only someone who was really crazy . . . or looked really crazy, really capable . . .' David picked his way round the piles of junk towards the rear doors in a high brick wall. 'These doors lock?'

'Locked right now,' said O'Rourke.

'And the street gates?'

'I close the two by padlock. From the outside, when I leave.'

David reached out, took the acetylene torch, and contemplated it. Turn the force of evil against those who generated it . . .

He said, 'Mr O'Rourke, will you telephone Mr Stimson and tell him you may have some payment for him.' It was an order, not a question.

'Will I hell. Where d'you think I can raise—'

'Raise nothing. Except the telephone. Just make the call, tell him you've got it here *now*, and leave the rest to us.'

'Us?' said Ronald King, dubiously as they crossed the road to his Rover.

As they drove to the offices of the minicab and Hercules companies, David explained what he had in mind. Part of it shook King so severely that he came close to driving the Rover up on to the pavement near a lamp standard. When he had regained control he gasped, 'You're mad. I should have known it.'

'You want them defeated. This is the way to do it.'

'Why couldn't we just sit and wait at O'Rourke's place and jump 'em?'

'They might be too strong for us,' said David patiently. 'It's essential to harass them a bit at a time. It's the cumulative effect that will work in our favour.'

They reached the corner of the street with five minutes to spare before Stimson and two of his thugs came round the side of the offices and got into a Jaguar parked on the apron. King held back as they set off on the return journey to the scrapyard.

'If I take our carrot-topped friend,' said David, 'can you handle two?'

'With my golf club,' said King dourly. 'The bit I don't like is wrecking this motor. It makes me sick to think of it.'

David was remorseless. 'Use the side that's already damaged.'

'All right in theory. But—'

'We have to anger them – build up their own force until they've lost control of it, and we can use it against them.'

'You'd better be right.'

King kept his distance from the Jaguar. It did not matter too much if they lost it for half a minute. They knew its destination. It was just a matter of timing their own assault.

Two hundred yards from the gate into O'Rourke's yard, King banked his foot down on the accelerator. The Rover surged forward alongside the Jaguar, then swerved inwards. The impact jarred through David's shoulder, but he kept deliberately, philosophically calm. It was not easy, as both cars mounted the pavement and screamed to a skidding halt. Out of the corner of his eye David was aware of King's stricken face and of a red blur beyond him: the Rover had come to a final standstill with a red pillar box crumpled over one wing. And it was not the hitherto undamaged side.

But King was wasting no time in recriminations. He was out of the car, grabbing a golf club from under the seat, and racing round to the Jaguar. Stimson erupted from the driver's seat, face to face with David Castle. David grabbed his nose and tweaked it hard. Stimson screamed, as much with the indignity of it as with the pain. Instead of following up this stroke, David turned and dashed along the street. Stimson came pounding after him. There was no time to check on how King was making out. David swung through the open gates of the scrapyard, slowing only when he was sure that Stimson was safely inside, too.

Outside, O'Rourke emerged from a neighbouring doorway, closed the gates, and padlocked them.

David turned to face Stimson again. Stimson, panting with rage, made a wild lunge. David, all his reactions meticulously timed now – all the time in the world, it seemed, just the way it ought to be – adopted an aikido crouch, let Stimson twice waste his energy against it, and then neatly twisted him over and down. Stimson lay on the ground, his fingers scrabbling, trying to push himself up.

David said, 'I am one half of Manor Debt. You have been trying to collect debts using violence. I won't allow that. You must go well away from this area, otherwise I shall be forced to use your own violence against you.'

Stimson lurched up like a wounded but dangerous animal and hurled himself forward again. David made a step back, jabbed, and threw his opponent back to where he had started. Then, taking Stimson's arm, he dragged him to his knees and urged him towards a metal bench where O'Rourke had left the acetylene cutter alight. With one hand David picked up the cutter; with the other, he forced Stimson's nose close to the oxygen cylinder beside the bench.

'Yesterday you put this flame against this oxygen bottle,' he said. 'I'm going to demonstrate to you now the reason why you will take your business away to another part of London. We are both going to see what happens when the flame is left against the bottle.'

He laid the flaring cutter in place.

Stimson struggled desperately. 'You're crazy. We'll burn alive. Let go . . . help . . .!'

The flame went on burning. The surface of the cylinder was discolouring. Stimson screamed louder.

O'Rourke opened the gates and came in, watching the scene, awestruck.

David said, 'You can go if I never see you again.'

'All right, yes . . . for God's sake, let me get out of here.'

O'Rourke stood back to let him race past, out into the street. When Stimson was well and truly gone, he came the rest of the way and turned off the flame.

'Now that was a lot of panic about an empty oxygen bottle, right?'

'Right,' said David. He became aware of another shape tottering into view round the edge of the gate. For a moment he tensed, awaiting another onslaught from one of Stimson's heavies. But it was Ronald King, taking a few paces and then sinking to his knees. David hurried to heave him up on his feet again. 'Are you okay?'

'Okay,' King croaked.

'I don't think we'll see Stimson again.'

'Good.' It was about as much as King could summon up. 'Good.'

Back at the office, King did not even dare to make critical remarks as David set to work pumping up the front tyre of his moped. The state the Rover had been left in, derisive remarks about any other vehicle would be hopelessly out of place.

After a few minutes David stopped pumping and stood up, puffing. The strain of the morning had taken it out of him. But it had been worth it. His muscles ached and his mind was still stretched taut; but he had been strengthened by the experience, and after a spell of meditation this evening – rather than another spell over the bottle with King – he felt there was a real chance of inner renewal.

A red mini coasted slowly along the other side of the street and came to a halt. Nobody got out. David had a keen sense of being watched.

He turned his head.

Deirdre opened the driver's door and looked challengingly at him.

David put down the pump and crossed the road. 'What d'you want? If it's about a possible appeal, I'd prefer to talk about it in office hours. Your office or this one, it's all the same.'

'Keep it impersonal, you mean?'

She was miffed, awkward, unsure of herself and of him. Which made two of them.

'I don't know that I meant that. Don't know at all.'

'I . . . David, I'm sorry. I should have stayed and talked. I thought I'd get after Parish right away, but . . . I mean, I should have known . . . there were more important things. Like you.'

'It's your job, isn't it? Isn't that what it's all about?'

'I've been wrong,' she said. 'And boring.'

He said, 'I've had rather a busy morning. I'm getting hungry. I'd like to take you out to lunch.'

A timid smile dared to tug at the corners of her mouth. He had forgotten quite what a delicious, vulnerable mouth it was. 'I'd like to be taken.'

Before he could go back to shove the moped indoors and tell King where he was going, an increasing engine noise round the far end of the street announced the appearance of a garage breakdown truck, towing what David recognized as the Rover, though it might have baffled others. It was not until the truck ground to a halt near the Manor Debt window that Deirdre cottoned on.

'Isn't that your friend Ronald's car?'

'It's been in a spot of bother.'

'I think you could say that,' she said with ill-concealed relish.

He hurried across to announce the arrival of the wounded vehicle to Ronald King. Deirdre followed at a more leisurely pace and waited for the two of them to come out again. King did so with some reluctance, made a dismal inspection of the distorted vehicle, and shook his head.

Deirdre said, 'You appear to have been in an accident, Mr King. Do you want me to pursue any legal claim against a third party?'

'Only this one.' King stabbed a thumb at David as if warding off the evil eye. 'I listen to him, I do what he tells me – and look at my motor.' He turned fearfully towards the driver of the truck, waiting for the worst. 'Well – what does Mr Balfe say?'

'We put it up on the ramp, Mr King. There's a lot of body crease. Requires complete centre shell. About a grand's worth of engine compartment incursion, plus new front sub frame.'

'Price?'

'Too much. The insurance won't pay. You take my advice, Mr King – take the write-off price.'

'I refuse to believe this.'

'What I'll do for you, I'll take it down to the breaker's yard to wait for the insurance assessor.' Before King could plead any further, he added, 'Gospel truth. You are looking at your motor on its way to that last great NCP in the sky.'

Deirdre, genuinely sympathetic at last, put a hand on King's arm. 'Cheer up. It's only a car. Only a way of getting from A to B.'

'I had that motor utterly immaculate for six years.' King glared at David Castle. 'Then you come into my life and it's one accident after another, ending in a write-off.'

Deirdre said, 'I'll take you both to lunch. On one condition.'

David looked full at her. She was taking on substance. She was becoming real, coming back to life again. Or maybe he was the one to whom that was happening. He said, 'What's that?'

She indicated the moped and then the truck. 'As the Rover's being carted away, that goes too.'

'Oh, no.'

It was the only thing that could have dredged King up from his slough of despond. His eyes brightened. 'Oh, yes,' he agreed. 'Perfect.'

'No.'

Gloom had been banished. King was ecstatic. 'This rusting rubbish counts for more than your girlfriend?'

'Who says she's my—'

'I mean it,' said Deirdre, her cheeks pink and her eyes blazing. 'It's me or it.'

David ran a hand through his hair, doing nothing to improve it. He was baffled: what was she offering, or not offering, or demanding . . . or waiting for him to offer? He needed time. Maybe he needed more time than she or anyone else would ever have. If she expected him to propose, right on top of what had happened in that courtroom . . . It was not the right time. He was not sure there would ever be a right time. His last attempt had been an appalling failure. Proposing to girls was a habit he didn't fancy catching.

King said, 'Turn the other way, young Castle.'

David refused to turn the other way. Like a condemned man too gallant – or too stubborn – to accept a blindfold at his execution, he stared as King lifted the moped bodily and heaved it over the edge of the truck.

'It worked perfectly,' said David. 'It was economical. That thing of yours was really wasteful . . . costly . . .'

'Here's a promise.' King watched the truck move away with its cargo of discarded transport. 'We need to sort a few things out. And a few people. But we're doing well enough. With the insurance write-off and a few weeks' hard work in certain quarters, I'm going to put a deposit down on two company cars.'

David could just see it. King with the big new one, and himself saddled with a four-wheel version of his lovely lost moped. Before he could express this in forceful language, Deirdre said, 'If you two will just stop brooding and get in my car, we can go somewhere and eat.'

David realized that he had spoken the truth earlier. He was truly, staggeringly hungry. He hesitated. King suffered no such hesitations. He strode towards the mini, opened the front passenger door, tipped the seat forward, and waved David towards the interior.

'In you go.'

'No,' said David. 'After you. You're in the back. I'm going in the front.'

King spread his arms, appealing to Deirdre.

'Both of you in the back,' she said. 'But don't start a battle behind my head. I like to concentrate when I'm driving. Saves a lot of twisted panels and cracked paintwork.'

King looked at David in outrage. He looked back, and grinned.

Women . . .! They both said it silently, chauvinistically.

'What a pair of wallies you are, you two.' Deirdre was smiling at them, at herself, at something still not found but perhaps just within reach. 'Hopeless.'

They drove off towards food, argument, and whatever else might be lying in wait.